# Sense &

# Sensibility

# 1N SPACE

# Sense & Sensibility IN SPACE

## Sybil Nelson

*Sybil Nelson*

Sense and Sensibility in Space  Copyright © 2018 Sybil Nelson

Published by Little Prince Publishing in Charleston, South Carolina.
Cover Design: Jessica Richardson of Cover Bistro

.

ISBN-13:  978-1-939947-09-3
ISBN-10: 193994709X

Printed in the United States of America
Visit www.LittlePrincePublishing.com

# Prologue

Leaven CoZark, a Regavite from the planet Kemek, eyed the patrons of the rathskeller looking for someone who could satisfy his fleshly urges. He hated his visits to AiJalon, especially the city of Cosmo. The planet as a whole was much too conservative for his personal tastes. Cosmo itself seemed to be the center of purity and chastity. It was almost as bad as Minnith where nearly every inhabitant was a priest of some sort.

If Cosmo was situated near a paedor, it would be a different story. He would be able to sneak away from his business affairs for a few moments to have his physical needs met. But as it was, he was too far away. He had to settle for a secret location where a few like-minded individuals gathered to partake of drinks and temptations. The problem was in options. This establishment in particular, located under the popular Parque Hotel, lacked variety. It held only about seventy-five people, more than half of whom were people just like him looking for satisfaction. Of the remainder, the women were completely tame compared to what he would find in a paedor. He wasn't even sure if there were any humans at all there tonight. He longed for some human companionship.

After letting his eyes wander around the poorly lit room for several moments, they finally settled on a pretty girl who had just been served a Gadolan fire iced tea. The flame from the drink highlighted something dark and dangerous about this girl. Instead of waiting for the flame on the top of the glass to subside as most people did, this girl placed her entire hand above the rim as if daring it to burn her. He allowed his eyes to wander down her body where he noticed that she was not wearing the monochromatic clothing units typical of people in Cosmo. Before he even realized it, he was walking towards her place at the bar.

"May I buy you a drink?" he asked, sitting next to her.

"Why? Do I look thirsty?" she asked in response while taking a sip of her drink.

He smiled. She was feisty. He was going to like her. "It is just the polite thing to say when you are interested in someone."

"Polite? Really? Since when do you care about politeness, Leaven CoZark?"

"Oh, I see you've done your research on me, young lady."

The girl nodded. "What can I say? I am really good at my job. You have no idea how good actually."

"I don't? Why don't you enlighten me?"

"I know everything there is to know about you," she said, leaning toward him.

"Really? Like what?"

"I know you are a wealthy businessman from the planet Kemek," she said as she leisurely traced a finger up and down his chest over his dark shirt.

"Well, that is common knowledge. Anyone who is anyone knows that about me."

"I know that you come to Cosmo twice a year, usually visiting Paedor III," she continued.

"Can you blame me? It is the finest paedor on the planet."

"And when you come to AiJalon, you never leave without a gift for yourself." Her voice changed slightly from one of seduction to one that seemed slightly angry. To CoZark, however, she still seemed to be providing foreplay. "A gift in the form of a young girl."

"Hey, that has never been proven—"

"And I also know," she continued, interrupting him, "that the hypnotic I slipped into your drink several minutes ago should be kicking in right … about … now."

Panic flooded every inch of his body as he noted he no longer had control of that body.

"You can't move your muscles, can you?" she asked. He tried to respond but he couldn't. "Don't worry. I can move them for you. Don't believe me? CoZark, stand up." Unable to control himself, he obeyed. "Very nice. CoZark, sit down." Again, he obeyed.

"Now let's do something more interesting. CoZark, bite your tongue so hard that it bleeds."

The girl smiled as a warm liquid trickled down his chin. He began to whimper.

"There, there. Don't cry. It's just a little blood," she said as she wiped his chin. She sighed. "How does it feel? How does it feel to have no control? To be at the mercy of another being for what happens to your own body?"

She looked at him pitifully. "What's that? You can't respond? How about we go upstairs to your room and explore these feelings a bit more? CoZark, stand up and take me to your room."

He obeyed and began leading her out of the establishment.

"Told you I was good."

# Chapter 1

Hin'Roy Dashing was an elegant combination of striking good looks, prudence, and general congeniality. The first twenty-five years of his life Hin'Roy spent in complete obedience to his parents. He always did what was proper, logical and pure just as a true AiJalonian should. This led to an adequate marriage that was efficiently arranged by his parents. Hin'Roy's life with his first wife was adequate, productive and satisfactory. They had one son and lived a rather comfortable life in a grand estate called Nova located on the island of Plymouth in the Castille Archipelago.

Hin'Roy felt he had a good life. He thought that he loved his wife. That was until she died and he met a human woman named Marzi. She was unlike anything he had ever seen or encountered. He didn't know what love was until he met her. And he quickly learned that a life could be much more than adequate, productive, or satisfactory.

He knew the laws about humans and owning property, but he also knew that he had one pure AiJalonian son who could no doubt care for any children from his second wife. Thus, when he and Marzi had three children, he felt confident they would never end up in a paedor.

Hin'Roy's oldest son, Bragley Dashing, had been amply provided for by the estate of his mother and had at the same time married very well. Financially, that is. In every other matter, Femili Fyatt Dashing was completely lacking. Things such as empathy, compassion and all other emotions she felt were too human and, thereby, beneath her. But unlike most AiJalonians, it wasn't always logic that guided her thoughts and actions. Femili Fyatt Dashing was guided almost exclusively by money and acquisitions of property.

So, it came about that Hin'Roy grew ill. As he felt the end of his life approaching, he summoned his firstborn son, Bragley. He needed to relay a message to him and a TelEx would not do. This had to be done in person.

"Father!" Bragley exclaimed upon seeing his father's condition. He had no idea his father had deteriorated so rapidly. It was just about of the Revuan Flu. People recovered from it all the time.

"I know what you are thinking," Hin'Roy said with a smile. "I look amazing, don't I? Like some sort of Pentaline singing sensation, eh?"

"Father?"

Hin'Roy began to laugh, which quickly turned into a coughing fit.

"Just a joke, Bragley," he said when he caught his breath.

Bragley didn't pretend to understand. His father had certainly adopted so many human qualities from his current wife.

"All joking aside," Hin'Roy began seriously. "I am worse than I look. Had I contracted this flu thirty years ago, I might have been able to recover quickly. But as it is now, I am much too old. I don't have much time left."

"Nonsense, Father. There are any number of drugs that can eradicate the Revuan Flu."

"And I have tried them all. None of them work. It is too late for me." Hin'Roy grabbed his son's hands. "But it is not too late for your half-siblings, and your stepmother. They have so much life ahead of them. Please make sure it is as pleasant as possible."

"I will, Father."

"Promise me."

"I promise."

With that settled, Hin'Roy felt secure in the knowledge that his family would be taken care of. He called for his wife and soon died in her arms.

Bragley Dashing was not a cold-hearted man. In fact, had he married a more amiable woman, he might have turned out to be almost as loving and caring as his father. After making the promise to his father, he had settled it within himself to let his half-siblings and stepmother continue living at Nova. He, Femili, and their son Hin'Rik certainly had no need for an extra home. They lived quite comfortably in Cosmo and Femili owned three other island homes across the planet.

Bragley smiled within himself at such a generous decision. Certainly, he would be thought of as a great and benevolent man.

Less than two hours after the passing of Hin'Roy Dashing did Bragley find his wife packing her belongings.

"My dear, I do not feel we need to take so many things for such a short trip."

"Short trip?" Femili asked without pausing in her motions. "Bragley, whatever are you talking about?"

"The funeral for my father is tomorrow. I suppose we could stay a night or two at Nova, but we should be back in no more than three days."

"Why on AiJalon would we return in only three days? There are so many improvements I plan on making to the residence that we will need to stay there at least a month. Even if I didn't want to make improvements, why would I want to leave our new home so soon?"

"Our ... new... improvements?" Bragley stuttered. Suddenly he remembered that he hadn't shared his generous intentions with his admittedly ungenerous wife. Now he didn't know how to even broach the idea of letting his half-siblings continue to reside at Nova.

"My dear, you recall the promise I made to my father, do you not?" he asked gently.

"Yes, yes. Will you summon a servant droid to pick up this case? It is filled."

Bragley pushed the call button then said, "Well, I thought it would be very generous of us to let them remain in their home at Nova. We already have a home here in Cosmo. Why on AiJalon would we need to move?"

Femili paused and stared at her husband as if he were some sort of alien creature. Suddenly she smiled. "Oh Bragley, you had me frightened for a moment. Are you attempting some of that human humor? Funny, my dear. I think."

"But, I wasn't ... "

"Surely, you wouldn't think of forsaking AiJalonian laws? Those laws are there for a reason. The law very clearly says that Nova now belongs to us. You cannot argue that fact."

"Yes, but ... I wonder."

"What dear?"

"Where will they live?"

"Well, in the paedors, of course. That is where all humans belong. It is a way of life they are used to. A life they enjoy."

"But I made a promise to my father that I would take care of them."

"What exactly did you promise him? What was the precise wording of the promise?"

Bragley thought for a moment. "I told him I would make sure their lives were as pleasant as possible."

"And there you go. As pleasant as possible. And what could be more pleasant for a human than life in a paedor? They get to live life in their familiar, debauched manner without fear of AiJalonian laws of decency. Really, life outside of a paedor must be very strange indeed for a human. I mean, think about it. In a paedor, a human is allowed to eat flesh, roam the streets naked and fornicate at will. What could be more pleasant for them?"

Bragley was speechless.

"Besides," Femili continued, "life in a paedor was obviously what your father intended for them. He left them a monthly rent allowance that could only allow them to purchase a home in a paedor."

Bragley wanted to explain that his father had left his human wife and children the maximum allowed under AiJalonian law. Humans were not allowed to own land or inherit money or property. A trust could be established to pay for living arrangements for a human but that trust had a monetary maximum. It was an unlucky coincidence that that maximum could only cover the cost of a small room in a paedor. Thus, by design, all humans were eventually relegated to the paedors unless they could marry someone of pure blood and, thus, be allowed to live in civilized society.

Most AiJalonians thought that allowing humans to live in a paedor was much more than they deserved. When humans first arrived on this planet, they tried to conquer it and enslave AiJalonians. The ensuing war was quick and quite embarrassing for the human population. All the AiJalonians had to do was adjust the magnetic core of the planet and all of the antiquated human weapons completely failed. Helpless and stranded on a foreign planet, the AiJalonians could have enslaved them or banished them back to their own dying planet Earth. Instead, the council decided to let them stay but under heavy restrictions.

After taking a deep breath Bragley said, "But they have only ever lived in AiJalonian society. How do you know they would desire to live that kind of life?" He couldn't even bring himself to say the word paedor.

"Oh, Bragley. You are precious," Femili said in a tone that translated to, "Oh, Bragley, you are an idiot." Then she kissed him on the cheek. That was the end of the conversation.

\*\*\*

So distraught was Mrs. Marzi Dashing about the behavior of her stepdaughter-in-law that she had on several occasions considered simply setting fire to Nova and all its belongings. It was only the level-headed counsel of her eldest daughter that prevented that from happening.

"Mother, you have never been a favorite of Father's family. Destroying the Dashing family home would do nothing to secure their affection."

"Elsinor, you are wise well beyond your twenty years," Mrs. Dashing said. "And it is completely infuriating," she added as she handed over the electronic torch.

Just then Madrick entered the parlor to find his sister holding the torch. "Oh, good! Elsinor is on board with the torching then."

"Very funny!" Elsinor said though, in truth, she wasn't sure he was actually kidding. "The two of you must behave while Femili and Bragley are here. We are at their mercy."

Madrick exchanged a devious glance with his mother. The two of them were too much alike: emotional, headstrong, impulsive, and well, human.

"When is the last time I have not behaved?" Madrick asked with a sly grin.

"When is the last time the suns have risen?" Elsinor responded.

"I deserved that. 'Twas a stupid question." Madrick kissed his mother and his sister on their cheeks then said, "I'm off for a ride on my new duster."

"New? You bought a new duster?" Elsinor asked. "You know we can't afford such expenses at this time. We have no idea what the future has in store for us."

"Relax, Elsie," Madrick said. "I didn't buy anything. I collected parts and built it from scratch."

"You mean that pile of metal that was in the side yard last week?" Mrs. Dashing asked. "You made another duster out of that already?"

"Yes, it is as good as new. Might be the best one I've made yet. I swear it's faster than the ones they sell on Lumerca. Care to come for a ride, Mother?"

"There is no time, Madrick. We have to pack."

"Elsinor? A ride?"

"Gaion, no. And don't say swear. It is not polite," Elsinor said. "Mother is right, you know. There is much to do. Our brother and his wife will be here any moment."

"All the more reason for me to leave immediately," Madrick said, putting on his riding gloves and practically running out of the room.

"Be back before the second sun sets," Elsinor called out after him. "Mother, you need to begin to reign him in. He is going to turn out positively wild."

"What would you have me to do with him?" Mrs. Dashing asked.

Elsinor sighed. "I don't know, but building and riding dusters is not respectable employment for a young man."

"Madrick is not your typical young man," Mrs. Dashing responded. "He is as beautiful as any AiJalonian in form and appearance, but as soon as he speaks, his humanity betrays him. Building dusters may not be respectable for a typical AiJalonian but there is not much he is allowed to do given his genetics ... my genetics." Marzi Dashing dropped the plate she was packing and immediately burst into tears.

Elsinor hugged her mother. "Don't cry, Mother." Elsinor often found herself in the position of comforter to every member of her family. Though she suffered deeply over the untimely death of her father and the expulsion from the only home she had ever known, she found that at twenty years old, she was more emotionally equipped to deal with the situation that her twelve-year-old sister, her nineteen-year old brother and even her mother.

Elsinor had inherited the calm, reserved, obedient spirit of her father. Thus, she was adept at concealing the powerful human emotions that sometimes arose in her. Madrick and her mother were so alike in temperament that it was sometimes difficult to tell that Madrick had any AiJalonian blood at all except for his striking looks. He had already captured the hearts of several young ladies based solely on his appearance. If it wasn't for his humanity, Elsinor felt sure he would have been long married.

Twelve-year-old Mahogany's true temperament was still in formation. So far, however, it seemed as though she was leaning more toward her human side.

# Chapter 2

Within moments of arriving at Nova, Mrs. Femili Fyatt Dashing had reprogrammed all the droids to recognize her as the mistress of the house instead of Mrs. Marzi Dashing. Femili Fyatt Dashing then spent the rest of the day evaluating and appraising every inch of all the twenty rooms in Nova. She visualized the new furnishings she would add and mentally calculated how much it would cost to transition Nova into the lavish island retreat she envisioned. Femili Fyatt Dashing absolutely could not wait to invite her Cosmo friends for a visit to the new Nova ... for a small fee of course.

"Nova has been quite well looked after during the past twenty years of human occupation," Femili said during dinner that evening.

The humans at the table stared at her with a mixture of shock and contempt.

"What?" Femili asked when she realized no one had thanked her for her observation.

Noticing the tension his wife's comment had created, Bragley quickly said, "She meant it as the highest of compliments."

Madrick glared at his half-brother. "If that was a compliment, you must need Engorian armor to suffer her insults."

Neither Femili nor Bragley could comprehend human sarcasm or rhetoric. They were at a loss as to how to respond. Maggie laughed at their discomfort which lead Femili to believe that Madrick's comment was merely a joke.

"Ah, that human humor," she said with a condescending smile. "I shall not pretend to understand. I am sure you will be so much happier around your own people. I am sure they will not only understand your jokes but laugh heartily. Something an AiJalonian is just unable to do."

"It wasn't a joke," Maggie began. "Madrick was insinuating that—"

"Thank you for the compliment," Elsinor said, interrupting her little sister.

"I may be human," Mrs. Marzi Dashing began, "and my children may be half-human, but we have lived as AiJalonians in this house for the past twenty years."

"That must have been very difficult for you," said Femili. "Having to repress all your human emotions and tendencies for so long. Imagine how much happier you will be when you are in your true home."

"True home?" Madrick asked.

"Yes, where you belong."

"You mean the paedors, don't you?" he asked.

"Well, of course."

"You expect us to live in the paedors?" Madrick was getting visibly angry. Elsinor's chest tightened. She couldn't even process the idea that her sister-in-law wanted to expel her from the regal estate of Nova to a filthy paedor. No, she would have to think about that later. Right now, she had to focus on calming her brother down. She placed her hand over his and squeezed it tenderly.

"Of course, you will live in a paedor," Femili said. "Where else on AiJalon could you live?"

"We could continue to live here if Bragley would allow it," Maggie said.

Bragley opened his mouth to speak but Femili was too quick.

"That is not possible, dear. And it is not at all what your father intended. Why, what he left you for rent will barely cover a dwelling in a paedor."

"That was all he was allowed to do by law," Madrick said. He didn't even try to conceal his anger and other emotions swelling in him.

"And who are we to subvert AiJalonian law?" Femili took a demure sip of soup. Elsinor held her brother's hand tighter for fear he would reach across the table and slap the spoon out of her hand.

"But Bragley promised he would help us. I heard his promise to his father with my own ears." Marzi Dashing spoke to Femili but stared directly at Bragley. Her voice trembled and she had difficulty finding the appropriate words in AiJish and thus slipped in and out of human English.

No matter the language she spoke, Bragley could not help but understand her meaning. Unable to hold her gaze, he turned away.

"What exactly do you think he is doing now? You are here, aren't you? We could have turned you out the moment Hin'Roy drew his last breath, but we did not. My husband is so generous that he is letting you stay probably for an entire month until you can get situated in your paedor. I don't see how you could expect more."

"All these years I wondered why you were never close to our father," Madrick said through gritted teeth directly at Bragley. "Now I understand. I am so happy he raised me to be a better man than you."

# Chapter 3

The dreadful dinner conversation from the night before played over and over again in Marzi Dashing's mind. She and her children would have to live in a disgusting paedor. It was the worst possible outcome she could imagine. Though she was human, Marzi had never actually spent any time in a paedor. She had grown up on Tentor where humans were treated with much more dignity than on AiJalon. Hin'Roy Dashing was on a business trip to her planet when they met and she fell passionately in love with him. It was that blinding emotion that allowed her to ignore the plight of humans on AiJalon and return to this planet with her beloved. Now, she didn't have enough money saved to return to Tentor. In fact, AiJalonian laws made it nearly impossible for her to acquire such a sum. People from her home warned her not to marry an AiJalonian because of their treatment of humans. Oh, how she wished she had listened. If she had to do it all again, would she? The past twenty years had been such happy ones, but were they worth the pain she was now enduring? Could she possibly live in paedor?

Those thoughts plagued her mind during dinner the next evening as she pushed the normally tempting rice and fried fials around her plate. Marzi Dashing couldn't stomach the idea of relocating her family to such a demeaning dwelling.

No one even attempted conversation for fear it would devolve into a repeat of the previous night.

Femili, for her part, was not concerned about offending anyone at the dinner table; she was merely tired of the ungrateful attitudes of the human Dashings. She briefly wondered if there was a way to somehow strip them of the surname along with Nova. Femili hated the idea of sharing her name with humans. It was only the fortune Bragley had inherited from his mother and the promise that one day Nova would be hers that allayed her discomfit of his human relations when they were married.

"I have good news for you all," Femili began toward the end of the dinner service, hoping to lift the spirits of all in the room. "My brother Edgar is to visit us tomorrow." Femili looked around the room, confused as to why there was not more excitement and thus decided to continue. "He is far and away the most eligible bachelor on the planet if you ask me. His only rival is perhaps my other brother Roymond."

"Must have been extremely tiresome for you to have met every person on the planet in order to be able to make such a claim."

"Madrick," Elsinor said while kicking her brother under the table.

"Well, I haven't met every person on the planet, but I can say that my brother Edgar speaks several languages, is exceedingly well-mannered and handsome and, let us not forget, he is set to inherit a great fortune from our mother. We expect many great things from him. Perhaps a position in the Ministry of Purity or the Ministry of Justice. He may even be able to marry into the royal line."

After such an introduction of Edgar from Femili, Madrick, Mahogany, and Marzi had resolved in their hearts to dislike him no matter what. Elsinor was much too sensible for such prejudgments and instead occupied her mind with thoughts of how to keep her family out of the paedors.

# Chapter 4

Early the next morning, Elsinor retreated to her favorite lake less than a mile away from Nova. She wanted to go for a swim in the inlet that was closer, but feared it would reveal her true feelings. She always went for a swim when she was upset. It was the only thing that calmed her nerves and returned her to her normal tranquil state. But going for a swim would immediately alert her brother and mother that all was not well with her. She didn't want to upset them further. She had to be strong for their sake. So, instead, she settled for sitting by the shore and staring at the rising second sun. It was in this moment of reflective solitude that she thought about her father and cried.

\*\*\*

Edgar Fyatt's journey from Cosmo to the Castille Archipelago had exhausted him more than expected. He sighed. Truth be told, it wasn't the journey at all but the mere idea of having to spend a week with his sister Femili that was completely exhausting.

"Pierre, stop flight," Edgar called to his droid pilot. The guster immediately whirred to a stop. Exiting his guster, Edgar drew in a long deep breath of the island air. Yes, this is what he needed, a few minutes alone in nature to meditate and ready his mind for his encounter with Femili.

Choosing a direction at random, Edgar began to walk. He observed and meditated on Gaion's creation and found peace. He was just about to turn back when he spotted a beautiful glowing lake and decided it was worthy of further inspection. Maybe he could see one of those sea creatures people were always going on about but that he had never had the fortune to encounter. As he approached closer, he realized he wasn't the only admirer of the lake. There was a woman sitting on the shore and she seemed to be crying. Edgar froze. He wasn't very good in these situations. He didn't have the best way with words and he was certain he would end up saying the wrong thing and cause the woman more harm than good. He turned to make a silent retreat when he stepped on a bundle of dried leaves.

"Is someone there?" the woman called.

Edgar considered pretending he didn't hear the entreaty and running back to his guster, but he thought that would make him look guilty of something. Having decided against fleeing in fear, his brain still hadn't registered the thought that he should probably turn and answer the question. He sensed the woman had stood and was coming toward him. He could hear her footsteps approaching but he couldn't force himself to move. Gaion! Why was he so awkward?

"Who is there?" she asked.

Finally, Edgar turned around and said, "No one of consequence I assure you." Apparently, that was the right thing to say. The woman smiled and wiped a tear away from her face. Her beautiful face. Her loveliness momentarily stunned him into silence. Thankfully, she spoke next so he didn't have to.

"I am so embarrassed," she said, composing herself further. "I don't normally show this much emotion. I am usually very poised."

"I am sure your expression of emotion is perfectly justified."

"Most AiJalonians believe public displays of emotion are never justified."

"Well, then, it is a very good thing that we are not in public and that I am not like most AiJalonians."

"Indeed."

Indeed. What did that word mean coming from her at this time? Did she agree? Was she pleased with his attempt at wit? Was she happy that he was not like most AiJalonian men? Was she uncomfortable with the fact that they weren't in public? He noticed that she was at least part human; maybe she feared decency laws since they were alone. Why did her presence make him doubt everything?

"May I escort you home?" Edgar asked, trying to fill the awkward silence.

"No, I am quite all right. I feel I should collect myself before returning home."

Edgar nodded but found he could not move. Logic told him he needed to turn and head back to his guster, but something else within him made him want to stand where he was and continue to watch as she went back to her spot on the shore. Part of him wanted to follow her, sit next to her and continue their conversation. He had never felt so comfortable talking to anyone before in his life. He would rather spend an hour with this woman he had just met than five minutes with his sister Femili. Femili. Oh dear, he was late.

# Chapter 5

Elsinor found she felt better after meeting the mysterious man on the lake. There was something about his nature that put her at ease. She wondered if she would ever see him again as she would very much like to.

Just as the second sun began to warm the waters to a fervent glow, Elsinor decided to return to Nova. She felt she had healed her emotions enough to handle a few more days with Femili. A few days. She would not be able to endure more disparagement from Femili. Any human living on AiJalon understood it meant living as a second-class citizen. Humans had to endure almost constant prejudice and injustice. The fortunate ones were able to carve out some semblance of a decent life especially if they married an AiJalonian and lived on the islands. That was the case with the Dashings. For most of Elsinor's life, being human wasn't a stigma because she was well provided for by a loving father.

But in an instant, all of that was now changed. Not only did she no longer have an AiJalonian parent to shield her from the prejudice on the planet, but the only home she had ever known had been taken away from her.

Elsinor was desperate to find a new place to live that was away from Nova but not too close to a paedor. So far, all the living accommodations that had come their way were far outside their budget. Somehow, her mother just could not fathom the idea that they were now very poor and would not be able to afford anything even close to the grandeur of Nova. After a brief prayer to Gaion, Elsinor began her walk back to Nova.

Upon entering the parlor at Nova, she was shocked to see the very same man she had met at the lake.

"Well, finally," Femili said as Elsinor entered. "We had no idea where you had wandered off to. We considered sending the intergalactic police in search of you but who knows how that would have turned out. You could have been arrested and completely embarrassed the Dashing name."

"What are you talking about?" Madrick asked. "She just went for a walk."

Ignoring Madrick, Femili said, "In any case, meet my younger brother, Edgar."

Edgar and Elsinor stared at each other in silence for an awkward moment as neither of them quite knew what to say. Should they pretend they had never met? Should they announce to all in the room that they had just met by the lake? Alone? Finally, prudent and quick thinking Elsinor broke the silence by saying, "Pleased to finally meet you officially."

"Likewise," Edgar responded.

Elsinor felt the eyes of all in the room staring upon her and she quickly looked away.

"I was just explaining to my brother how all the humans were looking forward to returning to a paedor," Femili said.

"Femili," Edgar said chastisingly.

"What?"

"How c—can one return to a place they have never b—been?" Edgar asked simply.

Suddenly, Elsinor realized that Edgar had a rather pronounced stutter. She wondered why she had not noticed it before.

Femili paused as if replaying the logic of her brother's statement in her head. Apparently concluding that she could not counter it she said, "Well, they are human so I am sure they will be much happier there."

"And you are a monster, so I am sure you would be happier in—"

"Edgar," Elsinor said, expertly changing the subject while interrupting what was sure to be a truly offensive comment from her brother. "How long can we expect your visit?"

"Just as long as I am welcome and no longer," he said to Elsinor. There was no stutter in his words. He spoke clearly and plainly. And Elsinor rather liked the timbre of his voice.

"Oh, you can stay as long as you like, Edgar," Femili said. "And shortly there will be a lot more room for you to truly enjoy Nova."

"Are you s—sure about that, F—Femili? H—have you even asked when the D—Dashings will be ready to leave the only p—place that has b—been their home for the p—past t—twenty years?"

"Edgar? What on AiJalon has gotten into you? You have never disagreed with me so openly before."

"I have never had the m—motivation before," he said, making eye contact with Elsinor.

"Hmph," was all Femili could say. Elsinor wondered if Femili noticed how her brother stared at her. If she did, she gave no indication. She just continued with what seemed to be some sort of sales speech about her brother. "Did I mention that Edgar is the oldest son? He therefore will be inheriting the majority of our mother's fortune. And it is quite a fortune. He is going to make some fortunate woman a very respectable and remarkable husband. Isn't that right, Edgar dear?"

"I highly d—doubt that, Femili. There is nothing q—quite remarkable about me."

Femili thought for a moment. She seemed confused. "But you are going to be rich. That, in and of itself, is quite enough to be remarked on. Thus, it makes you remarkable."

"If the size of one's bank account is the only thing noteworthy about a person, it goes without saying that the person must not be so special," Madrick said.

"This coming from someone who is poor," Femili responded.

"I'd rather be poor than mediocre or quotidian." Madrick stormed out of the room hoping that Femili didn't know what that word meant.

# Chapter 6

"Why did you lie to your sister?" Elsinor asked Edgar once they were alone.

"Lie? What are you talking about?" he asked.

"You made it seem like we had never met. But we did indeed meet earlier today at the lake."

"I never directly SAID we had never met. In fact, you are the one that offered the introduction between us first. So, if anything, you are the one who lied to my sister."

Elsinor thought about this for a moment. He was right. In order to not make the situation awkward, she was the one who said 'pleased to meet you.' Now suddenly she felt guilty for being dishonest.

Edgar apparently noticed her uncomfortableness.

"Now, now. Do not feel bad about it. It was an honorable dishonesty. I don't think my sister would have understood the situation. And, truth be told, it was none of her business that I stopped at the lake this morning. In fact, it was her disposition and manner of being that necessitated my reprieve. My sister drives me a bit mad."

"Is that why you stutter when you are around her and not when you are with me?"

Edgar thought for a moment. "Gaion, you are correct. I do not stutter around you. I am perfectly calm in your presence. I wonder what that means."

***

Elsinor didn't consider herself to be especially talented or gifted in any sense. When she looked at her younger brother and sister she marveled at their abilities. Madrick could immediately understand anything mechanical that he touched. One day, they discovered that talent also transferred to musical instruments when he found a broken bandalore, fixed it and then proceeded to delight everyone with his musical talent. That was also the day that they discovered Mahogany's dancing ability as she accompanied his music with her inspired dance moves. Elsinor felt positively mundane in their presence. The only thing that could remotely qualify as a talent in Elsinor's case was her ability to commune with nature. Whenever she went swimming, sea life big and small flocked to her. Even the skittish flicker fish who normally avoided humanoid figures would provide Elsinor with her own private light show in the water. She doubted her familiarity with fish would ever take her far in life. There was hardly a market for flicker fish tamer. But her ability provided her with ample entertainment when she went for her daily swim.

"May I join you?" Edgar said one morning before one of Elsinor's daily swims.

"Excuse me?"

"Oh, I'm sorry. I do not mean to be forward. It's just that Madrick tells me you have a way with the sea inhabitants. I just wanted to observe."

"You have an interest in things marine?"

"Actually, I do. I have lived on AiJalon, a water planet, and I have never in my life seen a flicker fish or even a dolphin."

Elsinor's eyes expanded. "You've never seen a dolphin? I can understand not seeing a flicker fish in your lifetime, but dolphins are everywhere." It was true. Humans had brought dolphins to the planet when they had settled on AiJalon after leaving Earth. And since they had no natural predators, they populated rapidly.

Edgar shrugged. "Maybe there's something wrong with me."

*There's nothing wrong with you,* Elsinor thought. *You're perfect.*

"You just have to know how to talk to them. Come, I will show you."

Fortunately, the grounds of Nova included a sea inlet that was in full view of at least half of the rooms. Thus, Elsinor and Edgar didn't have to fear violating any decency laws as long as they did not touch each other.

Edgar followed Elsinor as she stepped slowly into the water, her white dressing gown stretching behind her as if it were the train of an embellished wedding gown. He was sure she probably only swam in a bodysuit on normal occasions, but in her effort to be especially irreproachable around a member of the opposite sex, she wore a gown over her bodysuit. It was just as she ought to have done and it made her even more appealing.

"So, what do I do?" he asked as water lapped against his legs. He felt slightly underdressed in Elsinor's presence given that he only wore his tight-fitting bodysuit, but he tried to not let his discomfit show. "Is there a magic phrase or something to say?"

Instead of responding, Elsinor looked back over her shoulder. She smiled then pressed her index finger to her lips, the intergalactic symbol to be quiet. He wouldn't be able to speak again if he tried. He was struck silent by her beauty. Elsinor Dashing standing waist deep in iridescent water with a thin dressing gown cascading behind her might have been the most beautiful thing he had ever seen in his life.

Kneeling slightly, Elsinor brushed the tips of her fingers across the water in circular patterns. Then, as if the marine-life concurred with Edgar's assessment of her beauty and wanted to be near her as well, a school of fish swam right up to her. They were flicker fish! Each of the twenty or so little three-inch-long fish began swimming in circles around Elsinor. Seconds later, they started to glow.

"Gaion above!" Edgar exclaimed in as muted a tone as possible. "How are you doing this?"

Elsinor shrugged. "I don't know. They just like me."

Edgar understood why.

"Humans call this species Haliantha delbine." She spoke quietly so as not to disturb the fish. "I believe it comes from an ancient human language called Greek. It means 'sea bloom flower.' AiJalonians, however, call them Whalhium. Legend has it that the original twelve families on AiJalon used them to light the way toward food."

Mesmerized by the timbre of her voice, he hung on every word that came out of her mouth. He didn't want her to stop, but suddenly she did. After a sharp intake of breath, she looked up, out towards the sea. Then she smiled and said, "Here comes an old friend."

Edgar was completely confused until he followed her line of sight and saw the creature that had eluded him his entire life. A dolphin.

"This is Lutus," she said when the dolphin came close enough for her to touch. And then she did. She touched a dolphin! This was so contrary to everything he knew. AiJalonians admired sea-life and believed all the creatures were beautiful gifts from Gaion, but they also believed they were separate entities. They felt that humanoid creatures had no reason to interfere with them and interrupt their lives. On the other hand, humans felt that sea creatures were in existence for their pleasure. They were constantly exploited or eaten in the paedors. So, to see Elsinor approach this dolphin with neither of those philosophies was nothing short of extraordinary. She actually called a dolphin her friend.

"Lutus, this is Edgar," she said, speaking to the dolphin. "He's a friend. And how do we greet our friends?" The dolphin apparently understood exactly what Elsinor was saying. Amazingly, he lifted his head and torso out of the water. "He wants a hug," Elsinor said to Edgar.

"A hug? You want me to hug a dolphin?"

"Yes, you have to. Otherwise, he will be offended."

Nervously, Edgar approached the dolphin. And after a look of reassurance from Elsinor, he reached his arms around the dolphin and gave him a gentle squeeze. The dolphin made an odd sound and then splashed back into the water.

Smiling, Elsinor said, "He's happy to meet you."

"Oh, well, tell him the pleasure is mine."

Elsinor giggled. "He can understand you perfectly fine."

Directing his attention to the dolphin, Edgar said, "So sorry, Mr. Lutus. It is very nice to meet you as well."

The dolphin made another odd squeaking sound. Elsinor laughed again. "He says, no need for the 'mister.' Lutus is just fine."

"How do you know what he's saying?"

"He speaks a language just like any other. In some ways, it's easier to understand than Ancient Ai. In any case, Lutus and I have been friends for over ten years. In that amount of time, you can communicate with someone even without words."

Elsinor proceeded to hold an entire conversation with her dolphin friend as Edgar watched in awe. Gaion, what manner of woman was this Elsinor Dashing?

***

"I didn't know you played the bandalore," Edgar said later that evening. They had just had another contentious dinner with Femili Fyatt Dashing and had retreated to Madrick's room to ... well, hide. Edgar, in his attempt to find a way to run into Elsinor had found all the Dashing children together and decided to invite himself in.

"I don't really. I have never had any formal training," Madrick said.

"But he's amazing," Maggie said.

Madrick picked up the bandalore that sat in the corner of his room. It was an instrument that resembled an ancient guitar in form but sounded more like a wooden flute. It made a lovely, soothing sound. Madrick had learned to play at his youngest sister's request when she saw someone from Pentach dancing to it.

"He really is quite talented. Madrick just has a way of understanding how things work," Elsinor added. "It is extremely remarkable. If we had a ziln I am quite sure he would master that in a matter of minutes."

"You must be a genius," Edgar said.

Madrick shrugged. "Perhaps. Too bad being a genius doesn't eclipse being human. If it did, my family would be safe."

"Your family is safe."

Madrick shook his head. "Maggie, why don't you go get prepared for your performance for us? You can dance in your room. We'll be right behind you."

43

After his little sister left, Madrick continued. "You don't understand, Eddie. Can I call you Eddie?"

Edgar beamed at the thought of a nickname. He had never been close enough to anyone to warrant one.

He nodded and Madrick continued. "You will never understand what it is like to be part human. Our fate lies in the hands of people who either fear us or believe we are idiot savages who have no business interacting with their species. No matter what I do, good or bad, it is always somehow connected to my humanity. If I get upset at an injustice, I am just being an emotional human. Yet, if I excel in speaking one of the AiJalonian languages it is not because I am human it is in spite of it. I must have been well-trained by some scholarly AiJalonian. I can't win. And being a human male is even more stigmatized. I am supposedly inherently violent and belligerent. Any moment I could be accused of aggression and because I am human it would be easily believed. Then instantly, I would be exiled to a paedor or worse a prison planet and then who would care for my sisters and mother?"

Edgar so wanted to say that he would take care of them if anything ever happened, but he knew he could not truthfully make that statement no matter how badly he wanted to.

"So, forgive me if I don't feel that being building cars, fixing robots or playing any musical instrument that I touch has any bearing on my life at all."

An uneasy silence fell upon the room. Elsinor feared that Madrick's outburst had made Edgar too uncomfortable.

"I am so sorry for your troubles," Edgar said, looking down. "If there is anything I can do ..."

Elsinor eyed her brother. It was a look that said "fix it or I'll break you."

"So, I hear you met Lutus today," Madrick said, changing the subject.

"Yes, Lutus actually gave him a hug," Elsinor said, happy for the change.

"Wow. High praise indeed. Lutus is usually very picky about the men in Elsinor's life. He hates me for some reason."

"Madrick!"

"Not that you are a man in Elsinor's life in particular. I mean you are a man and—"

"Why don't you take Edgar to see some of the other attractions in the Castille Archipelago?" Elsinor said, interrupting her brother.

"Yes, that w—would be l—lovely," Edgar said. His stutter was back. Madrick had made him nervous.

"Really?" Madrick said. "What other attractions are there? He's seen our inlet, he's met Lutus and even a school of flicker fish. There is not much else."

"Well, what about the lake?" Elsinor asked.

"Yes, the lake is qu—quite a sight," Edgar said. "Very sh—shimmery."

"And?" Madrick asked crossing his arms. "What other sights are there to see in Castille?"

Elsinor thought quickly. She had lived all of her life in this archipelago and it was quite common knowledge that there was not much to see. Castille was by no means as stunning or splendid as other archipelagos on the planet such as Penuel or Juniper. The only other thing people came to visit in Castille was Nova.

"The Groely Dam," Elsinor said finally.

"The Groely Dam?" Madrick asked in disbelief. "A three-foot tall wall of mud? That is what you think he should visit?" Madrick shook his head. "Listen, Edgar, if you are interested we can go for a ride on a couple of dusters and I will show you the real Castille."

Edgar smiled. "Yes, I think I would like that very much."

Elsinor smiled as well, for she noticed that he had said the entire phrase without a hint of stutter.

# Chapter 7

"So, it really is a wall of mud," Edgar said, staring at the wall of well ... mud.

Madrick shrugged. "I told you." He removed his helmet and sat on the sand. "Just because I'm human and I CAN lie, doesn't mean I do. I find lying unnecessary."

"What do you mean?" Edgar removed his helmet as well and sat next to Madrick. Helmets were not at all the fashion and Edgar could see why. They did terrible damage to his mane of hair. But when Elsinor heard they would be riding that day, she made both of them promise to wear helmets. He couldn't refuse a request from Elsinor. Given his current situation, he would do all in his power to make her happy. Unfortunately, his power was not nearly as vast as he wished.

"What do I mean? Well think about it," Madrick said. "There can really be only three reasons to lie. One, lying for personal gain. Not applicable in my case. I'm human. There is nothing for me to gain."

Edgar wanted to dispute this, but he couldn't. It was true.

"Two," Madrick continued, "to save yourself from embarrassment. Or three, to save someone else from pain. Personally, the only people I am close enough to to want to save from pain are my sisters and mother. There is no need to lie to them since they know every little thing about me. Furthermore, lying to them in the present could perhaps bring them pain in the future. I would not want that."

Edgar felt the truth of those words more than Madrick could ever know. "And what about the first reason? Do you ever get embarrassed?"

Madrick shrugged. "I am human. My mere existence is an embarrassment to the majority of beings on this planet. At some point, you just have to embrace it and get over it."

"I wish I was more like you," Edgar said.

Madrick guffawed. "More like me? Are you insane? You are pure AiJalonian and you are rich. You have absolutely nothing to worry about. I, on the other hand, due to half my genes have no way of protecting those I love most. Do you know how emasculating that is? Nothing is more embarrassing than not being able to care for my mother and sisters. Thus, I can't imagine there would ever be a reason for me to lie to save myself from embarrassment."

"Believe it or not, I know what it's like to not have the freedom you desire. To not be able to make the choices you wish."

"No offense, Eddie, but you have no idea what humanity is like. I am completely trapped."

Unfortunately, Edgar did know what it was like to be trapped. Also, unfortunately, he was not at liberty to discuss the particulars of his entrapment.

"So, level with me Edgar," Madrick said, a few moments later. "Are you in love with my sister or not?"

"I am n—not at liberty to s—say."

"Not at liberty? What on AiJalon does that mean? It is a simple yes or no question about your own feelings. Surely you have liberty to feel your own feelings."

"When you are in my p—position, you do not. And if you value our friendship at all, I b—beg you to not press the situation any f—further."

Madrick didn't need to press the matter any further. He knew the truth. He could tell by the way Edgar looked at Elsinor. By the way he seemed to come alive whenever she entered a room. By the way he never stuttered when she was around. He knew Edgar was in love with his sister whether he was 'at liberty' to say so or not, whatever that meant.

\*\*\*

"Well, what did he say?" Mrs. Dashing said to Madrick later that evening. "Were you able to find out anything? Does he love her? Is he going to propose? Are we all saved?"

"I don't know."

"You don't know? How can you not know? The whole purpose of you going riding with him was to discover whether he had any real affection for your sister Elsinor or not. I cannot believe you failed."

"No, the purpose according to Elsinor was to show him around Castille. It just happened to coincide with your purpose as well. And I wouldn't say that I failed, Mother. I determined that he does not NOT love her. But something is holding him back."

"So he is not going to propose?"

Madrick sighed. "I can't say one way or the other. I think he wants to, but familial pressures may be too much for him to bear."

Now it was Mrs. Dashing's turn to sigh in defeat. "I guess I cannot conceal this offer from her any longer," she said, holding her personal receiver. It held a TelEx from a distant cousin of her late husband.

"I think Elsinor will think the offer from Comte Middleton is more than adequate for the three of us," Madrick said

"Oh, I am sure she will. I just want to hold off as long as possible, especially if there is a romance developing between her and Edgar."

# Chapter 8

"Marzi, may I bend your ear for a moment?" Femili asked as they both watched Elsinor and Edgar walk around the perimeter of Nova. By Femili's count it was their third trip around. Why on AiJalon would they need or much less want to walk around and around the property? Their seeming intimacy troubled her.

"Why yes, of course," Marzi said, taking a seat next to Femili on the balcony. "May I just say that we are so happy to have met your brother Edgar? He is a fine young man."

"Indeed he is," Femili said. "And he has so much potential. The Fyatt family expects a great many things from him. As the eldest brother he has very many responsibilities."

"And I am sure he will fulfill those duties masterfully. And with the right mate, he will exceed every expectation."

"Interesting that you should mention the right mate," Femili said, staring at Edgar placing his coat around Elsinor's shoulders. "Our mother has very particular requirements for anyone who would marry Edgar."

"Well, I would hope your mother would also take into consideration Edgar's preferences and feelings."

"Feelings have no place in the logical execution of the Fyatt distribution of wealth."

"Excuse me?"

"The Fyatt family has a certain reputation to maintain. A level of purity that must not be tainted. And if it is, my mother is ready and able to withdraw every kind of financial support from Edgar."

"I see."

"I don't mean to offend. But let me be clear. If Edgar were to decide to marry a human, he would be cut off completely from the family fortune. So any young woman trying to trap him with her seductive ways is going to be sorely disappointed."

"I see," Marzi Dashing said again, standing. She stared at her daughter Elsinor. Seeing the light in her eyes that Edgar had brought made her equal parts happy and pained. "You think Elsinor is trying to trick Edgar into marrying her. And you are warning that such a course would result in poverty for the both of them."

"Good. Very good. I was not sure how well humans could understand the intricacies of—"

"Prejudice?"

Femili gasped. "I am not prejudiced. I am merely stating the way things are. The way Gaion or whoever created them."

Femili was not the most religious of people. Her only God was money. But she was rather persuasive. And persuasive people often had the ability to use whatever argument necessary to deliver their point.

Part of her didn't care. What did it matter if Elsinor and Edgar would be poor? At least they would be happy. But she knew that the more likely outcome would be that Edgar would never marry Elsinor. No one was that crazy to relinquish such a fortune. And even if he did, one small lover's spat could make him regret such a decision. She didn't want her daughter to feel like she was a mistake for the rest of her life. That was no way to live. Marzi knew that oh too well.

Sure, she knew that Hin'Roy loved her immensely, but it couldn't have been easy for him being married to a full human.

"Madrick, where is my receiver?" Marzi Dashing asked, stepping into his room. "I want to respond to Comte Middleton right away."

"And what will you be responding?" he asked, handing over the device. He had just been giving all the family devices software upgrades since he wasn't sure they would ever be able to afford new ones again.

"I am responding that we will be accepting his offer. We should be in our new home by the end of the week."

"This seems a bit rash, Mother, even for you. Have you discussed this with Elsie?"

"There is no need. I am the mother. Not her. I have made my decision and it is final."

Madrick could tell that his mother was not in the best of moods. He knew he needed to tread lightly. "So are we no longer concerned about giving Elsie time to get to know Edgar better?"

Marzi sighed. "I don't think any amount of time would be enough. Femili has made it quite clear that Elsinor is not good enough for her brother."

"But what about what he wants? He loves her. I'm sure of it."

"As am I. But I think it better for all of us to leave before Femili has a chance to poison Edgar against her and all of us. Perhaps, he can come to visit us in Haran. Then maybe they can continue their romance there."

# Chapter 9

Dinner as usual was painfully quiet except for the ramblings of Femili and her plans to refurbish and reestablish Nova as the premier visitation location of the Castille Archipelago.

When Femili paused long enough, Marzi saw an opportunity to make an announcement.

"We will be leaving by the end of the week," she said simply.

Both Edgar and Elsinor looked up from their plates in shock.

"We will?" asked Elsinor.

"To where?" asked Edgar.

"Oh, lovely," said Femili. "Did you find a nice little dwelling in a paedor?"

Edgar glared at his sister.

"No, Femili, we will not be living in a paedor," Madrick said. "But if you think the dwellings there are so nice, I invite you to live there. Maybe you can refurbish a nice little paedor dwelling for yourself."

Staring at Madrick slightly confused, Femili said, "You do not like me very much do you, Madrick?"

"Ya' think?"

"What does that mean?" Femili asked her husband. "I swear it's like these creatures are speaking a different language."

"We are moving to Haran."

"Haran? That's almost clear across the planet," Edgar said.

"But not too far for our friends to find us," Madrick said.

"And how long have we known about this relocation, Mother?" Though she directed her question to her mother, Elsinor looked directly at her brother. She felt betrayed that he hadn't mentioned this to her. They never kept secrets from each other.

"Last week I received a letter from my husband's cousin, Comte Middleton."

"Oh, a comte," Bragley said. "That sounds promising."

"He is offering us a domicilio on his property."

"Oh, a domicilio. Those are so adorable. You will be quite snug there."

"Yes, Femili. We are quite looking forward to four people sharing a three-bedroom domicilio while three people live in twenty-bedroom Nova. Part-time, might I add."

"A domicilio in Haran is still beyond your means," Bragley said, trying to draw attention away from Madrick's scathing remarks.

"How will you manage it?" Femili asked, "I mean, there is no extra money for you ... in the will that is." Everyone knew the true meaning of her remarks. She was implying that they would not be helping the human Dashings in any monetary way. Even though the promise Bragley made was to help his stepmother and half-siblings.

"He is not charging us the full price," Marzi Dashing said, staring directly into the eyes of her stepson. "He felt bad for our situation and felt the call of Gaion to help make it right."

"Oh," was all Bragley could say.

\*\*\*

"How could you not tell me about this?" Elsinor asked Madrick after dinner.

"This is not on me, Elsie," he said. "Mother wanted us to wait so that ... "

"So that what?"

"Well, you and ... "

"Me and ... ?"

Madrick sighed.

"Mother thought that if you had a little more time here with Edgar that ... "

58

"Oh, she thought maybe we would fall in love and get married or something?"

Madrick nodded. "And she is partially correct. You do love him, don't you?"

Elsinor took a deep breath. "I do not deny that I admire him and greatly esteem him," she said.

"Admire him? Greatly esteem him?" Madrick said, indignant. "Dear Elsinor, I have said kinder words in regard to my floset wrench."

"Fine, believe my emotions to be stronger than my choice of words but beyond that you must not allow your imagination to wander."

"Then there is no agreement? You are not engaged or not even in a mutual flirtation?"

Elsinor was at alarm. "No, whyever would you think so?"

"Why would I think so? Why wouldn't I? I have seen the two of you together. You spend every free moment in each other's company. You two are so in love. Anyone can see it."

"Love isn't enough sometimes," Elsinor said.

"Love isn't enough? Are you mad? Love is all there is. It's always enough." Madrick sat down next to his sister and wrapped an arm around her. "I am convinced that Edgar loves you. And given the right opportunity, he will ask you to be his bride."

Elsinor wondered what that opportunity would be.

The next day, as Elsinor and Madrick helped Maggie pack her belongings, they all heard a gentle knock on the door.

"Come in," Maggie called. Her face lit up when she saw it was Edgar. "Edgar! Can we take a ride in your guster? You promised."

"Oh ... I ... um," Edgar stuttered awkwardly as his eyes conspicuously avoided meeting Elsinor's.

"Before you go on that promised ride," Madrick said, filling the void that Edgar's stuttering did not, "I want to inspect the ... um ... levitation system. Make sure the rain didn't affect it." He stood and indicated that Maggie should come along.

"Rain?" she said, confused. "It hasn't rained in three days. Why would—"

"Never mind that just come along," Madrick said.

"Why? Why should I come? I know nothing of levitation systems and I do not care to."

"Well, you may need it for your future career."

Visibly confused, Maggie said, "What on AiJalon does dancing have to do with—"

"Never you mind, Maggie." Madrick picked up his little sister and playfully tossed her over his shoulder. Her shrieks of delight filled the halls as they exited the room, leaving Edgar and Elsinor alone.

He paced around the room a bit as if collecting his thoughts.

"There are many things to say to you..." Edgar began finally. "There are so many things I WISH to say to you." He paused as if not knowing what to say next.

Elsinor could hardly control the rate of her heart. Was he about to propose marriage? No, not marriage. It was too soon. They had only known each other for less than two weeks. In just those few days, however, she had felt closer to him than any other man she had ever met. And if he did propose marriage she would instantly accept. But Edgar was an AiJalonian gentleman to the core. He was all that was dignified and pure. A marriage proposal to a half-human after just a few days acquaintance would be viewed as highly unusual and possibly unacceptable. Perhaps he was about to propose a mutual flirtation. Elsinor would even be agreeable to that, though she would probably have to ask her brother for suggestions in how to behave. Though a year younger than her, he knew much more about mutual flirtations than she did. How much more, she never attempted to determine.

Edgar took a deep breath and then continued. "From the first moment I saw you ... on the lake ... I ... " He stopped again. "This week here at Nova ... with you ... has been the happiest time of my life."

"Mine as well," Elsinor said as she eagerly anticipated his next words. She imagined he was getting closer to revealing his feelings.

"There was a time in my life when I was not so happy. It was when I was a boy of fifteen. My own father had just died. I was ... filled with emotions I did not understand."

Elsinor nodded. She knew exactly how he felt. But she wasn't sure where his line of conversation was headed.

"My mother sent me away to school in Plyon. Have you heard of it?"

"Plyon?"

"Yes."

"No."

"Oh. Well, it is not far from where you are moving to in Haran."

A short silence fell between them for a moment until Edgar added, "I was there for two years. I was idle. And emotional. And confused."

"Understandably so. Your father had just died."

"He was a great man," Edgar said wistfully. "He was wise, practical, and reasonable. He judged people on their character and not their species." Looking at Elsinor he added, "He would have ... loved you." The way he said those last words were as if he was saying he loved her. But if that is what he wanted to say, why didn't he?

62

Edgar closed his eyes and shook his head. After opening his eyes again, he placed a small box on the table and said, "This is for you. I must leave now," then rushed out of the room.

In the box was an old-fashioned photo album. Inside the album were pictures of various lakes around the planet. The first lake was, of course, the lake where they met. Photo albums, actual photo albums with real pictures, were so illogical and impractical. Who would take the time to print actual pictures of locations and then configure them in a book to carry around? It made so much more sense to have the pictures electronically. But as she turned from picture to picture, she realized the sentiment in actually holding and touching the pictures. She then noticed the message written to her on the inside cover. It was written with real ink, like from a pen. She hadn't even seen a pen in years. Edgar must have gone through great trouble and expense for this gift and then to write the caption,

*Whenever you are alone or sad, sit next to a lake and know that I am near you if not in person, then in spirit.*

*Forever your friend,*
*Edgar*

# Chapter 10

"So? Any news," Madrick asked his sister when they were next alone.

"I have nothing to report."

"Nothing? Then why did he want to talk to you alone?"

"Who says he did? He came into Maggie's room. He knew I wouldn't be alone."

"But he came to her room looking for you. I could see it in his eyes. He had to have said something."

Elsinor shook her head. "Nothing of importance. He just wanted to say goodbye."

"How very odd," Madrick said. "I bet Femili got to him. That woman is toxic. But not to worry. When he comes to visit us in Haran, I am sure her effect on him will have worn off and he will propose to you then."

Elsinor wasn't so sure. There was definitely something very odd about Edgar's demeanor and Femili might not have been the cause of it.

***

The islet of Haran was located southwest of Cosmo between Plyon and Aphek. Haran was too large to be part of an archipelago but it was too small to be its own district. Thus, it was more of a private islet usually only visited by relatives of the residents. It was quite far from Castille. They had to hire two different gusters and finally transfer to a tobulin. Femili was ever so divided as to whether or not to help the Dashings pay for the expense of the move. On the one hand, it meant departing with money, an event she never liked to confront. But on the other hand, it meant being rid of them for good. In the end, she convinced her husband to give half of what would have been needed to make the full journey. Due to Femili's lack of knowledge of AiJalonian geography, Elsinor was able to convince her that Haran was twice as far as it really was. Thus, the sum Bragley provided turned out to be just enough.

Elsinor was immediately enamored with the islet of Haran. It reminded her very much of Castille. It was beautiful, quiet, and isolated like much of Castille was. Right away she spotted a lake where she would be able to sit alone with her emotions and quite likely think of Edgar.

The tobulin rode past what Elsinor assumed was Comte Middleton's home as it was the largest home they had seen so far. The structure was as grand as Nova, but had nothing of its charm. Barton was stately and modern while Nova was designed in the old style similar to the stone dwellings on Tentor. Less than a mile past the large home of Barton Hall they came upon what she assumed was Barton Domicilio. Domicilios were usually only visitor homes, built to house family or friends that were too annoying to stay in the main house for extended periods of time. It was much smaller than Elsinor had imagined, but to her surprise, it was a stone dwelling similar to Nova. Her heart swelled. It was as if it were a sign from Gaion. Her family could be happy here.

Marzi Dashing had thoughts quite the opposite to those of her daughter. To her, Barton Domicilio seemed impossibly small. Tears and emotion welled inside of her as she thought of how far they had fallen. How much they had been reduced to living in a home that was practically the same size as the hutch where Madrick used to keep his used droid parts.

Madrick's thoughts were somewhere in-between those of his mother and his sister. "At least we are not living in a paedor," he said, squeezing his mother's hand.

Before they could properly settle in or even evaluate in full their new home, they received their first visitor.

"Good day, good day, good mourning, good morrow. May your day be filled with goodness not sorrow!"

Maggie gasped. "That's Sirvinio Devas!"

"No Maggie," Mrs. Dashing said. "You are mistaken, this is our cousin Comte Middleton."

"Do not correct this little light of mine," Comte Dashing said bowing to Maggie. "For from her lips the truth doth shine."

"Mother, Srivinio Devas is a famous performer from Pentauch. He dances and sings and plays the ziln and the bandalore. Comte Middleton just spoke lyrics from one of his songs!"

"Oh, well, I was unaware."

"Do not fret, for it is not a sin. When what we do not know is far from within."

Maggie squealed. "Briton Metters! She's my absolute favorite! You know Briton Metters, too?" Then suddenly they both burst out into spontaneous song. It would have been adorable had it not lasted too long and become incredibly annoying. Neither Madrick, Elsinor, nor Marzi had any idea Maggie was so well-versed in music from other planets.

"Mahogany Dashing, how exactly do you know this music so well?" Elsinor asked.

"I told you I want to be a dancer. Dancers have to know music."

"Yes, but globe boxes and venabins are illegal. How exactly do you get an opportunity to even hear such music?"

Madrick cleared his throat. "I might have rigged her TelEx receiver to pick up entertainment feeds from other planets."

"Excellent, Madrick. You are going to get your little sister arrested for indecency before she even turns thirteen."

"Sorry, Mother. That was not my intention."

"Well, before we are all sentenced to jail, you must come dinner at Barton Hall without fail."

Madrick, Elsinor, and Marzi looked at Maggie, waiting for her to call out the name of some celebrity who sang the phrase in a song but Maggie just shrugged. "No idea who said that," she said.

Then Comte Middleton said, "That rhyme was all mine. I do that from time to time."

Though exhausted from the journey, the Dashings couldn't quite turn down an invitation from their generous benefactor.

"I don't understand why we cannot take the tobulin to Barton Hall," Mrs. Dashing said.

"Because this tobulin may very well be the last one we ever own. We have to keep it in good working order," Elsinor said. "There is no need to take it such a short distance when we can just as well walk."

"But if anything happens to our tobulin, Madrick can fix it," Maggie said.

Madrick smiled smugly. "You know she's right, Elsie."

"Oh, for the love of Gaion. I guess I am outvoted."

When they arrived at Barton Hall, a drone showed them to the dining room where Comte Middleton awaited them.

"May I introduce my wife and children four," he said. "If it were up to me we would have more."

"I am Comtesa Cai'ana Middleton," she said with a bow. "So pleased to meet you."

Elsinor found herself relieved that the elegant and relatively young comtesa before her didn't speak in rhymes as well.

"I can see it in your eyes," the comtesa said. "You are relieved that I am not rhyming as well."

Elsinor did not know how to respond. Yes, it was true she was quite relieved but she didn't want to say that for fear it would offend the comte. She in no way wanted to offend him considering the great generosity he was providing her family.

"It's okay to admit," Comtesa Middleton assured her. "I am keeping a running tally of people who are annoyed by the constant rhymes in hopes that one day he will yield to majority rule."

"And how do you fair?" Elsinor asked.

"Well, we have been married for thirteen years and I still have to put up with this ... " She paused in time to hear her husband say, " ... And tonight we shall gorge on fial pie. A sumptuous treat no one can deny."

"And does he always rhyme in English?"

The comtesa nodded. "Apparently it is easier to rhyme in human English than it is in AiJish or Ancient Ai."

Elsinor silently wondered if that was part of the reason why he was so willing to have humans rent his domicilio and at such a reduced rate.

The comtesa picked up two glasses of wine from a passing droid. "Here, this helps," she said, handing one to Elsinor. "The only thing more infuriating than my husband's manner of speaking is the way my mother adores it. Just wait."

Seconds later, the comtesa's mother made a grand entrance down the staircase, a resplendent, flowing gown trailing behind her. It was a gown that was a bit too formal for a family dinner. Elsinor wondered if she dressed like this all the time.

"Introducing Mrs. Jensent," a droid said followed by the sound of electronic clapping. The Dashings looked at each other confused and then joined in the clapping. Comte Middleton also clapped even louder than the droids. The comtesa snagged another drink and finished it in a gulp.

"May I introduce to you ladies and gent, the mother of my bride, the lovely Mrs. Jensent?"

An awkward silence followed in which the Dashings were unsure as to whether they were to clap again or not. To break the silence, Elsinor stepped forward and bowed a greeting.

"Mrs. Jensent, was I not right? Is not this beautiful family such a delight?"

"Yes, yes they are!" Mrs. Jensent said enthusiastically. "I am so pleased you are with us. J'ao, give me something that rhymes with pleased."

Comte Middleton thought for a moment and then said, "To rhyme for you will make me quite pleased; I must always keep the mother of my lady appeased."

Mrs. Jensen squealed in delight. "Ahh! He did it again. I swear, Cai'ana, this husband of yours is a genius."

Cai'ana smirked before taking another gulp of wine.

"So, tell us the story of your lives one and all as we sit together as family here in Barton Hall."

"Our story is very simple you see, for our home was taken from us three," Maggie said enthusiastically. Both Mrs. Jensen and Comte Middleton clapped in appreciation for her rhyme. Her brother, however, gave her a look that essentially said if you ever rhyme again I will disown you.

"Well, we know that dreadful business," said Mrs. Jensent. "And we are just so happy we could help you and save you from living in a paedor. What we really want to know—"

"Don't say we because I don't really care," interrupted Comtesa Middleton.

Undaunted, Mrs. Jensent continued, "Well, what my son-in-law really wanted to know is what is the story of your attachments? Surely, you don't want to live with your mother forever—"

"Trust me. You don't," the comtesa interjected.

"As I was saying, surely you don't want to live with your mother forever here in Barton Domicilio. Which means that you must marry." Mrs. Jensent set down her spoon and leaned toward Elsinor. "Tell me, do you have any prospects?"

"Lots of women like Madrick, until they find out he's human," Maggie volunteered. "That usually ends the relationship. But Elsinor has found someone that doesn't mind her humanity. He loves her anyway."

Both Madrick and Elsinor glared at their little sister. "Mahogany Dashing, you must not say such things," her mother scolded.

"Why not? It's the truth."

"And I can tell by her glow that there is more indeed to know," Comte Middleton said as he stared at Elsinor.

"Tell us, tell us now. We must have the full story," Mrs. Jensent said, about to burst with enthusiasm.

"There really is no story, there is no such person," Madrick said, trying to help his sister who was obviously too uncomfortable to even speak.

"But there is."

"Maggie, not now."

"If there is a story, it must be told. We are all friends. Do not fear to be bold."

"I have a story for you this time. I have a gulp of wine every time you rhyme," said Comtesa Middleton with a smile as she carefully brought a glass to her lips as if afraid she might spill.

"That was not a very good rhyme, dear," said Mrs. Jensent. "It didn't really flow. You should leave the rhyming to your husband, you know. Oh my, that rhymed." Both Comte Middleton and Mrs. Jensent burst into uncontrolled giggles.

The Dashings thought, well, hoped at least, that the rhyming and speaking in verse was just a temporary thing, but it continued for the rest of the evening.

# Chapter 11

The comte kept rhyming while the comtesa kept drinking. At one point, Elsinor was afraid the comtesa might slip into some sort of alcoholic coma right there at the dinner table.

"You know, dear son-in-law," Mrs. Jensent said, "even though Elsinor is apparently taken, I think we may be able to do something for young Madrick."

Madrick's eyes expanded. Elsinor knew exactly what he was thinking. Any woman these two could possibly recommend would have to be a completely inappropriate and possibly horrifying choice for a mate.

After thinking for a moment, the comte said, "Yes, yes, I think I know your thoughts. A mate for Madrick shall be sought. And not too far will we have to look. For soon a woman will steal his heart like a crook."

"You really think Maddie is going to fall in love?" Maggie asked.

"Oh, you can be sure of it. Once J'ao makes a prediction through rhyme, it always comes true," Mrs. Jensent said.

Seconds later, the bell sounded, indicating there was a visitor.

"Who could that be at this hour?" Mrs. Jensent asked.

"I forgot to mention that I invited Val over to stay with us for a few days." Comtesa Middleton leaned toward Elsinor and in a soft voice added, "When you are in my situation, it never hurts to invite an extra sane person or two whenever possible to try to counteract this lunacy. It goes without saying that you and your brother are always welcome."

"Miss Valdosta Greer, I am so happy you are here," the comte said.

"It's a pleasure to see you again, J'ao," said a tall AiJalonian woman who instantly captured the attention of the room. A silence befell all as apparently everyone needed to drink her in. The woman was relatively young but had what seemed to be an air of experience enveloping her. She seemed wise beyond her years and rich beyond all means as indicated by the color and stitching of her monochromatic clothing unit.

"Sorry, I didn't have time to change," she said when she noticed everyone staring at her. She looked down at her leg momentarily and that was when Elsinor noticed her injury.

"What happened to your leg?" Comtesa Middleton asked impertinently.

If the woman was embarrassed or abashed by such a question, she didn't show it. "I was injured slightly while visiting the planet Capernica."

"Slightly? Injured slightly?" the comtesa continued without restraint. "Your foot and the bottom of your leg is missing for Gaion's sake."

"Yes. It happened about a year ago. Which shows how much I have failed in maintaining my friendships," the woman said graciously. "It is so good to see all of you again after so long."

The room fell silent again. Perhaps everyone needed a moment to think of the most appropriate thing to say at this point.

Maggie leaned toward Madrick and whispered, "Who would visit Capernica? Isn't it a planet of thieves?"

He shrugged. "Might explain why they stole her foot."

"Dashings, Valdosta Greer," Mrs. Jensent said by way of introduction. "For all intents and purposes, Val can be considered my third daughter. She went to school in Cosmo with my youngest daughter Chai'loi but somehow seemed to hit it off quite well with Cai'ana instead."

"Perhaps because she realized Chai'loi is a complete lunatic just like the rest of you," Cai'ana remarked. Because she said it in ancient Ai, the humans in the room were able to pretend they didn't understand what she said while the AiJalonians in the room responded with different variations of "That was incredibly rude" and "You are drinking too much" also in ancient Ai.

"I am Madrick Dashing," Madrick said as he stood and gave a bow. "Allow me to introduce my sisters and mother."

Madrick often found himself in a very difficult position. In AiJalonian culture, it is the firstborn who would take the lead in introducing the family. In human culture, it was often assumed the man should take the lead. Elsinor and Madrick were so close in age that they would often take turns in taking the lead or let who had the greatest feel on the situation do so. Neither of them ever really minded who was in charge.

Val bowed in return. Then after taking a seat next to Cai'ana, she unceremoniously removed her wine glass from in front of her. "You won't be needing this anymore. I don't care what comes out of your husband's mouth," she said to her friend in ancient Ai. Elsinor noticed that Madrick had to stifle

a laugh because in ancient Ai, that phrase rhymed
perfectly.

# Chapter 12

After dinner, Val retreated to her quarters to change out of the confining Cosmo clothing unit and into a more comfortable island gown. Part of her wanted to remain in her quarters for the rest of the evening but that would have negated her whole purpose in visiting the islands in the first place. She needed to reconnect with old friends and reevaluate her purpose in life.

"I take it from your reaction that you and your brother speak ancient Ai," Val said later that evening to Elsinor Dashing.

"Was it that obvious?" Elsinor said with an awkward smile. "We were trying to hide that ability. We didn't want anyone to be embarrassed."

Val shrugged. "I am not sure embarrassment is a familiar emotion among this group."

Elsinor stifled a giggle by taking a sip of wine. "Does your mother or sister speak the language?"

"My mother can recognize a few words and Madrick and I are currently teaching Mahogany. Time will tell whether she has an affinity for it."

"Affinity for what?" Madrick said, joining Val and his sister.

"Affinity for language," Val answered in Ancient Ai.

"I was just telling Val that we are teaching Maggie."

Madrick smiled and Val felt her heart flutter in her chest as never before. "Yes, I wish she was familiar enough with the language to understand your joke. It was absolutely hilarious how you made your rebuke of Cai'ana rhyme."

Val wanted to say something else witty but found that she couldn't find the words. Thankfully, Elsinor spoke. "It kind of reminds me of some of your clever rebuffs toward Femili."

"Femili?" Val asked with a little more interest than she intended.

"Our half-brother's wife," Elsinor said.

"Yes, she is our sister all right," Madrick said using the Engorian word for sister which sounded almost exactly like the Ancient Ai word for a foul-smelling beast with two-heads.

Val laughed so hard she almost choked on her wine.

"You see, Val thinks it's funny," Madrick said.

"It may be funny now, but not when you say it directly to Femili's face, dear."

Madrick shrugged. "She doesn't speak Engorian so she had no idea what I was saying."

"But she does speak Ancient Ai."

"But she doesn't know I do. She probably just thought I was butchering AiJish."

"Or perhaps she wondered why there even exists a word for a foul-smelling beast with two-heads," Val said.

Madrick chuckled. "She wouldn't be alone. I've often wondered the same thing," he said.

"And have you reached any conclusions?" Val said.

"Why yes, of course. That word was obviously created several thousand years ago in expectation of horrible sisters-in-law such as the one and only Femili Fyatt Dashing."

"But those ancients would also have to predict the development of the Engorian language as well as the existence of wickedly clever brothers-in-law such as yourself who would know precisely when and how to use the word," Val said.

Val and Madrick shared a moment of mutual appreciation that kind of made Elsinor feel she should remove herself from the conversation. Unfortunately, her brother was blocking the only path of direct exit, making a natural departure impossible.

"So, what happened to your leg?" Madrick asked suddenly.

"Madrick!" Elsinor exclaimed. "I don't think that is an appropriate question."

"No, it's fine," Val said, tapping her metal prosthesis with her cane. "It was an accident."

"Well, naturally," Madrick said. "I do not expect you would purposely cut off your own leg."

Elsinor was about to scold her brother again for his impertinence but then noticed that Val was smiling. Unbeknownst to her, Val actually found Madrick's inquisitiveness charming.

"No, I did not cut it off myself," she said simply as if daring him to ask further questions.

After taking a sip of wine, Madrick said, "You are rather rich."

"And how do you know that?"

"Your demeanor, the color and stitching of the monochromatic clothing unit you were wearing. Shall I go on?"

Val shook her head. "Is the size of my bank account a crime?"

"Certainly not. But it is intriguing."

"And why is that?"

"I find it puzzling as to why a woman of your wealth would continue with such an economical prosthesis when with a simple tissue sample, you could have an entirely new leg grown on Lumerca and attached in a matter of days."

Val nodded as she looked down at her leg. "You are correct. My resistance to obtaining a replacement leg is not financial. It is personal."

Madrick stared at Val and she found herself feeling uneasy under his gaze. It was as if he could see things in her that no one else could.

"I don't pretend to know the true circumstances of your situation. But to me, you seem like a clever, independent and perhaps even nonconforming AiJalonian woman. Why let something hold you back when it doesn't have to?"

Val was stunned into silence. What manner of man was this Madrick Dashing who could read her like an unencrypted TelEx?

"What on AiJalon are you three talking about over here?" Mrs. Jensent asked. Val was most grateful for the intrusion as she had no idea how to counter Madrick's eerily accurate estimation of her.

"Nothing of consequence," Madrick volunteered.

Mrs. Jensent looked skeptical but thankfully chose not to press the situation. "I hear from your younger sister that you are quite the musician, Madrick Dashing," she said. "We have a lovely bandalore that never gets played. Why don't you bless us with a concert?"

"I'm really not very good," Madrick said. "I've never had formal lessons."

"He says that every time, but he really is amazing," Mahogany offered. "You have to hear him. Please play, Maddie. Please." She ran to her brother and cemented her request with an embrace.

Madrick sighed. "Oh, I can never say no to this one," he said, returning her hug. Taking up the instrument, Madrick began plucking it quietly in order to put it in tune.

"Wow, you already sound better than my husband and he's had that thing for ten years," the comtesa said.

"Cai'ana, really, he hasn't even started," her mother said.

Given that Madrick himself admitted that he hadn't had formal training on the bandalore, Val did not expect him to play so wonderfully. But she was beginning to realize that Madrick Dashing was nothing she could ever expect.

Madrick began strumming the bandalore confidently, filling the room with the warm, rich tones of the instrument. He chose a slow, soothing song that seemed to lift and sway the room as if it rolled along the sea. Finally, he added words.

What had Gaion done? Val thought to herself. How could a sound so beautiful come out of a face and physique so attractive? It was simply not fair.

Elsinor recognized the words and the language. Madrick often liked to write poetry in little known languages so that no one would know what he was actually saying. This poem was written in human Romanian and was perhaps the only thing on the planet that could make the music he was playing more beautiful.

When the song finished, everyone sat in a stunned silence. Mrs. Jensent even wiped away a tear.

"Madrick," his mother said, "I had no idea you sang as well."

"Just something I've been playing around with for the past few weeks."

"Won't you play us another one, please?" Mrs. Jensent asked.

"Well, I'm off to bed," Val said suddenly as she stood.

Everyone stared at her in shock. Surely, she couldn't want to leave the room when there was a chance she could receive a similar serenade.

"Are you sure?" Elsinor asked. "My brother has many songs he can play and rarely has opportunity for an audience besides his sisters."

"Quite sure. I am quite sure." Val had already reached the stairs. "But don't let that stop all of you from enjoying Madrick's ... Madrick's talents. I really must go."

*\*\*

Once in her private quarters, Val took deep breaths trying to calm her racing pulse and fierce heartbeat. What was happening to her? Oh, she knew what was happening. It had happened before. She had felt this way about someone else. It was something she hadn't felt in a year and a half.

Val took a seat on the bed while relieving herself of her island clothing. She momentarily missed the dress of the paedors. It was much more freeing. But she wouldn't dare wear the typical paedor pants and blouse that she normally would while on her missions. She couldn't let anyone at all know that that was where she spent most of her time. Except for Cai'ana, all the Middleton's knew was that she traveled a lot. With the amount of money she possessed, Val could certainly afford to travel anywhere she wanted. Most of the time, however, she wasn't traveling far at all. Just from paedor to paedor, helping people in any way she could.

It was in a paedor where she met her first love Milo. He was part-human and part Pentach. His easy smile, quick wit, and incredible talent meant he was more suited to succeed his family throne of celebrity back on his home planet. But instead, he joined a higher cause with Val and fought alongside her for two years. They had talked about getting married, and soon. But there was always another girl to save, another mission to carry out. And then it was too late.

A year and a half after his death, he was still all she ever thought about. Until Madrick. She shook his name from her head as if thinking of Madrick was somehow disrespectful to her dead fiancé.

Lying down on her side, she took out a holocube. She pressed the inset button and a three-dimensional image of Milo appeared. Val rested her head next to his, and cried herself to sleep.

\*\*\*

"So you sing as well," Elsinor told her brother after his performance.

Looking past her toward the stairs he said, "I've just been playing around with it lately."

"Really?" Elsinor asked as she followed her brother's line of sight. "And you chose tonight to debut a new talent?"

"Um, where did Val go?" Madrick said, finally revealing what was really on his mind.

"I'm not sure."

"Did she disapprove of the song?" he asked.

"How could anyone disapprove?" replied his mother. "Truly, Madrick my boy, your music was emotionally stirring."

Elsinor noted how Madrick did not seem satisfied with this response and continued looking toward the stairs.

# Chapter 13

Val could not stop thinking about Madrick Dashing. She felt an urge to be around him, to talk to him, to hear him sing. To that end, she decided to buy him a gift. But in order to divert suspicion of her growing feelings toward Madrick, she bought gifts for all in the Dashing family.

"This is very kind of you, Miss Greer, but I do not read music. I think you overestimate my talents," Madrick said.

"I thought you might say as much," Val said, producing a disc. "This is an ancient recording of an artist playing this exact song. I thought you would be able to listen to it and learn the music that way." Val plugged the disk into the receiver and the holographic image appeared. Madrick immediately seemed mesmerized by the music. All in the room knew it was the perfect song for him.

"Thank you, Miss Greer. I think I know how I plan to spend the rest of the day."

"I also have gifts for the other Dashings," Val said, willing herself not to stare into Madrick's magnificent face any longer than appropriate.

"Really? What?" Mahogany exclaimed.

"Mag, decorum," Elsinor chastised.

"Elsinor, I think she is allowed to lose a little decorum once she sees my gift to her." Val pulled out a painting from her bag. After handing it to Mahogany, she erupted into delighted screams.

"Good Gaion, what is it child?" Marzi Dashing asked.

"It is an autographed portrait of Srivinio Devas!" Mahogany screamed.

The older Dashings stared at Val with a mixture of shock, confusion, and disbelief.

"What? I heard she was a fan," Val answered their looks.

"But how—" Elsinor began.

"He was a friend of a friend and on a visit to Penteuch, I helped him out with a ... situation. This was a way for him to say thank you."

"Look, Mother," Mahogany exclaimed. "It is on actual paper with actual ink and there is his actual signature!"

"I am in ACTUAL amazement," responded her mother.

"And now it's your turn, Elsinor," Val said. "I have heard you had quite a friendship with a dolphin while you were on Castille." Val handed Elsinor a package. "This is an oxygenated body suit for swimming. The latest technology from Lumerca. It will allow humans to stay in the water longer than usual. You can swim longer and farther and perhaps go find him."

"Miss Valdosta, that is so incredibly considerate," Elsinor said.

As the women were speaking, Madrick wandered off and began strumming the opening notes of his new song. Silently, Val approached him and stood at his side. When he hesitated, Val used her cane to point to the proper string he should play next.

"Do you play?" Elsinor asked also approaching them.

"No," Val said. "I play the ziln a little. I don't know much about the bandalore. Only what a friend taught me once."

Val grew quiet for a moment as if the mention of this friend had caused her a degree of pain. "Well, on that note, I must say goodbye for a while."

"You are leaving?" Maggie asked. "Where are you going?"

"Mahogany, don't be rude."

"No, it's quite all right. I am headed off-planet for, um, business."

All wanted to ask her which planet she was going to and what business she needed to attend to, but they also knew it would be completely inappropriate.

# Chapter 14

Madrick mastered the piece of music given to him by Val in a matter of days. The Dashing women never tired of hearing him play the tune and often requested it several times a day. It was during one of these impromptu concerts that Elsinor innocently asked about her brother's interest in Val.

"Val and me?" asked Madrick confused at Elsinor's inquiry. "There is no possible way that Valdosta Greer has any interest whatsoever in me."

"I would not be so sure," Elsinor said. "You two hit it off pretty quickly. You must admit that she is a match for you intellectually."

Madrick shrugged. "I admit that I did enjoy talking to her. And her gifts to each of us were quite thoughtful."

"And she is very pretty and very rich. You must admit those things as well," said Marzi Dashing.

"Yes, all of that is true," Madrick admitted. "But none of that matters. She has no interest in me as evidenced by how she left the room when I started singing at Barton Hall."

"You cannot assume anything from that," Elsinor said.

"I agree," their mother said. "Perhaps she wasn't feeling well that evening. Maybe her prosthesis was causing her pain."

"And that is another thing," Madrick said, standing. "When is the last time you saw someone with a prosthesis that cheap and ancient? It is just odd."

"Once again," Elsinor said. "We cannot make assumptions as to her reasoning."

"And what about her leaving the planet?" Madrick asked. "If she had any interest in me, she would have stayed and gotten to know me better. How do you explain that?"

"I can't explain it," Elsinor said. "You should talk to her and ask further details. She seems apt to tell you."

Elsinor and Marzi shared a knowing glance.

"What was that?" Madrick asked.

"What?" Marzi and Elsinor said in unison.

"That look. Why did you look at each other like that? Do you know something?"

"We didn't look at each other in any special way," Marzi said.

"There. There you did it again."

"All right fine," Elsinor said. "It's just that Mrs. Jensent commented on how well you and Val looked next to each other which made Comtesa Middleton comment on the fact that she has never heard Val speak of another man the way she speaks of you."

"Really?" Madrick asked. "Well, we can't really make any assumptions based on that. Maybe she speaks ... ill of me."

Elsinor shook her head. "No, I don't think so."

"But you are not sure, are you? I am human. I cannot pursue a pure AiJalonian woman based on rumors and suppositions. Do you want me to end up in prison?"

Madrick had a good point. "Well, my son, just don't rule out the possibility," Marzi Dashing said. "It is possible that she cares for you. And it would be a good match."

"Possible, but not likely."

Madrick went for a ride on his newly restored duster in order to forget about Val, but she would not be forgotten. Valdosta Greer. Sure, she was pretty, and rich, but she was AiJalonian. Pure AiJalonian. There was no way he would put his heart on the line once again for an AiJalonian. Twice in the past he had fallen for women who were for all intents and purposes unattainable. Something in him believed that they had feelings for him but really, they just wanted a 'human' experience. A fleshly fling to satisfy some curious physical desire leaving him feeling hurt, used, and so cheap sometimes he felt he deserved to live in a paedor. No, the next time he fell in love, it would be a sure thing. It would be with someone who didn't hide their feelings behind ceremony and propriety. Someone who was forthright and not afraid to come right out and say how they felt. Someone who was willing to virtually strike him over the head with their love.

Just as he thought those words, he felt a strike to his person. Something crashed directly into him, throwing him from his duster and into a field.

Madrick landed awkwardly on his back and immediately felt excruciating pain. Though he surely had at least one broken bone, he was more concerned for the fate of his new duster. He forced himself up on his elbow where he could get a good look at the twisted lump of metal that was moments ago his pride and joy.

"Mitch!" he exclaimed, calling the name he had given it.

"Who are you? What do you want from me?" he heard a woman's voice say. For the life of him he could not understand why the woman was so angry.

"What are you talking about?" he asked as he painfully pivoted his body to get a good look at his accuser.

"Who are you and who sent you? What do you want from me?"

Madrick was still trying to catch his breath when she added, "Was it Ridgely? Did he send you? If so, you should tell him he's going to have to be a bit cleverer to catch me."

When he heard an odd click, Madrick looked up and was finally able to get a look at the woman. He was struck silent at her beauty. She was beautiful not because of her AiJalonian heritage, but in spite of it. There was a dark danger and a bright excitement that accentuated her striking features.

"Don't make me ask you again," she said when he didn't respond to her inquiry. "Was it Ridgely?"

The momentary trance Madrick felt by her beauty was suddenly overruled by annoyance and shock as he realized the click he heard was an equalizer.

"I have no idea who Ridgely is. And even if I did, I am in a great deal too much pain to— Great, Gaion! Are you driving a classic Mercedes Rover, Earth model from the year 2341?"

The woman's unwarranted anger abated slightly as she asked, "You are familiar with Earth cars?"

"Familiar? I am obsessed. I have always wanted to get my hands on one. I've read so much about them I think I could almost build one from nothing.

She lowered the equalizer and said, "Well, you must not be too obsessed because you are wrong. This car is from 2312."

Madrick thought he noticed a hint of flirtation in her voice. He smiled. "Doesn't matter. I could still give it the Mitch treatment."

"Mitch?" She raised the equalizer again. "And just who is Mitch?"

"Mitch. He was my best friend until you killed him."

"And exactly when was I to have done this? You have no evidence." Instantly, the woman's anger returned.

"No, no. You mistake me. Mitch is my duster." Madrick gestured behind him to where Mitch lay, a smoking heap of rubble. "I built him practically from nothing."

"Oh." The woman's eyes darted around quickly as if she was surveying her surroundings for danger. Then suddenly, she clicked the equalizer again and shoved it into a pocket inside a fold of her gown.

If Madrick was in his right mind, he would have wondered for longer than a brief second as to why an AiJalonian was carrying such a weapon, but as it was, the impact of the crash and the remarkable beauty of his assailant had effectively vanquished any such reasonable thoughts. With great difficulty, Madrick rose to his feet. The pain was excruciating but he refused to seem feeble in front of her.

"Are you all right?" she asked.

"Fine. Perfectly fine." He took a step forward and his leg collapsed. As he fell, the woman reached out to catch him.

"You don't look fine," she said. "Well, in all honesty," she added with a smile, "everything about you does look rather fine except for your leg which is admittedly my fault."

She was definitely flirting and the warm sensation her words gave him made the pain in his leg bearable. Well, almost bearable. "'Fine' might be a slight exaggeration, but at least I am alive. You could have killed me with your car."

"It wasn't my fault. Something is wrong with it. I lost control of the steering."

"Did you disengage the TMS?"

"The what?" she asked, still holding him up.

"Throttle Magnetization System," he said. "Help me over there and I will explain." Together they made the slow trek the twenty feet to the car. "Many cars from the 2300s were built to support a maglev system that was instituted for vehicle transport on Earth," he began to explain. "But since the magnetic cores of Earth and AiJalon are completely different, it can't be used effectively on this planet. Sometimes the steering will just lock up completely. If this was a car sitting in a museum for the past 200 years, I bet it hasn't been disengaged."

"Interesting," was her only response as she stared at the Mercedes.

"I could fix it for you in a matter of moments on two conditions."

The woman paused in thought for a moment as she helped Madrick lean against the car.

"Given that I almost killed you, I suppose I can grant you two small requests."

"Who says they will be small?" Madrick said, flirting in return.

She smiled. "Very well. I grant you two requests, big or small."

"First, I will need a ride home for Mitch and myself," he said.

"Agreed. And?"

"And I will need to know your name."

The woman smiled sweetly. "I'm Willow. Willow King."

\*\*\*

Madrick was indeed able to fix the car in a matter of moments. But a working vehicle was not motivation enough for them to want to leave each other's company. They spent the next several hours engrossed in conversation.

"Oh, I agree the Jungalor from Lumerca is a fine car, but it really has nothing on the Ferarri

Testarossa," Madrick said. "That just might be the greatest car ever created.

"A Ferarri Testarossa the greatest car every created?" Willow asked in shock. "Are you sure my car did not strike you in the head? For you are either misled, horribly mistaken or terribly ill."

"And what would you say is the greatest Earth automobile?" Madrick asked.

"Oh, it would have to be the Shelby Cobra. There is no question in the matter. I recently acquired a computer-generated rendering of one from the year 1963."

Madrick's eyes lit up. "Are you serious? Images of those creations are extremely rare."

"My father was a collector. He traveled the galaxy finding images of classic automobiles from several different planets. His favorites ... our favorites ... always came from Earth."

From the sadness that suddenly filled her eyes, Madrick knew something must have happened to her father. He wasn't sure if he should ask, however. Thankfully, he didn't need to.

"He and my mother died four years ago in a guster crash while they were of-planet." Willow sighed as if the memories were almost too painful to discuss. "I was too young to inherit property or fortune, so I was sent to live with my aunt and uncle in the Penuel Archipelago."

When Willow didn't provide any further information, Madrick attempted to lighten the mood.

"I hear Penuel is very beautiful. It is waterfall country, is it not?"

"Penuel means nothing but pain for me and I wish to never speak of it again if possible."

"I understand that completely."

"You do."

Madrick nodded. "Before I came to Haran, I had a beautiful home in the Castille Archipelago called Nova."

"You are the Dashings of Nova?" Willow asked, surprised. I have heard of it. Nova is a beautiful home."

"Yes, it is. But I no longer wish to speak of it. It was taken from me just because I am part-human. I didn't ask to be born human. Because of a situation I have no control over, I am reduced to living one step away from a paedor."

Willow was visibly upset at the sound of the word paedor. Abruptly, she rose to her feet and said, "The second sun has almost set. We should probably get you home."

# Chapter 15

Though Madrick took great pains to walk as normally as possible so as to seem strong in front of Willow, the few steps from the Mercedes to his front door were almost enough to subdue him.

"Gaion! What happened?" his mother exclaimed as soon as she saw the pained expression on his face.

"I assure you I am quite fine," Madrick said bravely.

"He keeps using that word," Willow chimed in. "Either he is unsure as to what it really means, or he is completely delusional and stubborn."

"Who is this woman and how does she know you so well?" Elsinor asked with a smile.

Madrick glared at his sister.

"I'm Willow," she said before Madrick could respond. She gave a ceremonial bow to all the women before adding, "I am afraid I am the cause of his injuries. I assume complete responsibility and, of course, will pay for any medical attention needed."

"I do not need medical attention," Madrick said stubbornly. "And if I do, we are equipped with a medical droid that is perfectly capable of fixing me up properly."

"Oh Madrick," Willow said with a teasing grin. "I didn't mean ... " She paused. Though she felt oddly close to Madrick after just a few hours' acquaintance, it was highly inappropriate to address him so informally so soon. The old Willow King, the little girl unaware of the horrors of the paedors, was completely consumed with the social norms of polite society. Over the past three years, however, she had abandoned nearly every aspect of her pure AiJalonian upbringing. But for some reason, she found herself wanting to make a good impression on Madrick's family. Willow forced the smile away from her lips and in the most conventional voice she could muster said, "Mr. Dashing, I did not mean to insinuate that you were incapable of attending to your own medical needs."

"It's all right, Miss King," Madrick assured her. "I am not offended. And while I may be slightly underestimating the extent of my injuries, let me assure you that I would gladly repeat them if it meant meeting you again."

"Madrick," Elsinor scolded at the inappropriate comment. He most certainly shouldn't be saying something like that to a strange woman he had just met. "We better get you inside."

\*\*\*

Madrick hobbled inside. Once past the door, he grabbed Elsinor's arm for support. "Is she gone?" he asked.

Maggie peeked out the window. "No, she's just standing there with this odd look on her face."

"Odd? How do you mean odd?" he asked.

"Maybe it is a look of confusion as to why a human would be so blatantly flirting with her," Elsinor said.

"Flirting? Me? Whatever do you mean?" If his family could have heard any part of their earlier conversation, they would realize that he did a lot less of the flirting.

"This isn't a joke," Mrs. Dashing said. "You were definitely flirting. You just met her! If Miss King is so inclined, she could most certainly charge you with felony flirtation."

"She's getting in her car and driving away," Maggie said.

"Oh, thank Gaion," Madrick said before collapsing to the floor. "My leg. I think it's broken."

Elsinor knelt beside her brother and began to feel for the bone. Madrick screamed in pain. "What are you doing?"

"I'm checking to see if it is broken!"

"I just told you it was! Are you trying to kill me?" he said, trying and failing to wiggle out of his sister's grasp.

"Well, what happened to being 'quite fine'?" she asked.

"I said that for Willow's benefit," he said. Madrick tried to relax on the floor as his little sister brought him a pillow. "I didn't want her to feel any guilt for our accident. Isn't she an angel of Gaion? And, oh how she knows her Earth cars. Not only does she know them, but she loves them almost as much as I do. She has an entire collection of them passed down from her father and she talks in detail about each one!"

"Well, she doesn't know enough about them to drive them properly," Elsinor said.

"That was due to a simple oversight in the operating system of the vehicle. It could have happened to anyone."

"And why did you tell her we have a medical droid?" Elsinor asked. "You know quite well we do not."

The bliss of romance had momentarily numbed any discomfort long enough to describe his angel. But now the pain of his injury was beginning to overtake him. "Just bring the service droid. I'll reprogram him or something," Madrick said with closed eyes and through gritted teeth.

"You are in no state to be reprogramming droids," his mother said, entering the room with a crystal cube to place on his injury. Neither Madrick nor Elsinor had even noticed she had left the room.

"Just rest and we will figure something out."

# Chapter 16

Willow tossed off her ornate island dressing gown as soon as she entered her parents' estate, opting instead for tan pants and a linen shirt. She felt an odd combination of feelings and needed to be comfortable in order to explore them. And nothing comforted her more than a little target practice in the field behind her home.

While firing a second round from her latest equalizer, Willow began to pinpoint some of her emotions. She felt excited, intoxicated, and stimulated. She didn't know she could feel any of those emotions outside of one of her missions. These emotions were due to Madrick Dashing. She felt ... feelings for him.

Considering her past, she never imagined that was even possible. The last time she thought she was in love it was with Ge'or Wixsum. A man who sold her to slavers. Not the best introduction into the ways of love.

Over the past three years, through her missions throughout the galaxy, she learned how men and women were supposed to interact. And, of course, she had the memories of her parents. She knew her parents loved each other, but outwardly, their emotions were quite sedate. Most likely due to their AiJalonian genetics.

Willow had spent quite a bit of time on Engor, and even though that was the home planet of her captor, she found herself admiring the passion and intensity of their romances.

Suddenly, Willow's equalizer stopped working. She cursed in Minnithian. The Minnithites, the most devout and religious race, ironically had the best profanities. Willow rushed inside to perform some calculations. There had to be a way to figure out when and how the AiJalonian core would be adjusted thus disabling all equalizers. She had spent so much money on new equalizers over the past month on the planet that it was becoming a burden. She needed to figure out the amount of change in the magnetisms in order to adjust her current equalizer accordingly or at least determine when the change would occur so she would know before being in the heat of battle when her equalizer would be ineffective.

Her calculations were not adding up. Sitting down in a lounge with a huff, her thoughts drifted to Madrick Dashing again. And not because he was the

111

most beautiful man she had ever seen, or because she had never been so at ease talking to another individual in her life, but because she recalled how he was able to disengage the Throttle Magnetization System of her Mercedes in a matter of seconds. Thus, he was obviously skilled with the necessary magnetization mathematics to solve her equalizer issues. All at once, her desire to grow closer to Madrick took on a twofold purpose.

Returning to the field behind her home, Willow took out several knives and began lobbing them at a tree. She prayed a brief prayer of forgiveness to Gaion for harming another living thing, but she really needed the target exercise and her equalizer was not an option.

As she expertly aimed the projectiles, she wondered if she could really do what she had planned in her mind. Could she use the apparent attraction between her and Madrick Dashing to her own personal advantage? Thinking about her mission from Gaion, she really didn't have a choice. She had to do whatever was necessary.

# Chapter 17

The Dashings never really figured anything out with regard to their lack of a medical droid. They merely tried to make Madrick as comfortable as possible with crystal packs and pharmaceuticals while Elsinor and Marzi attempted to reprogram a droid. It was a complete disaster. Madrick tried to help as much as possible, but as soon as they were at a tricky part of the process, Madrick would inevitably pass out from pain only to wake up seconds later wondering why they weren't done yet. Then he would spend the next several minutes talking about Willow before he could focus enough to help with the reprogramming only to pass out again before any real work got done. It was a maddening cycle that lasted well into the evening.

"Madrick, please let us at least ask the Middletons to use their medical droid," Elsinor said the next day.

"No! Absolutely not," he said. "It's completely embarrassing to have to beg for assistance. Give me one more drug and perhaps a shot of stimulant so I can stay awake and finish this."

"It is not sensible for you to suffer in pain when the Middletons will be perfectly amenable to us using their droid."

"I don't need assistance from anyone."

Before Elsinor could protest any further, the domicilio chimed, indicating a visitor.

"Are you all right?" Val asked, entering the Dashing cottage with Comte Middleton right behind. "I heard about your accident. You could have been killed."

"But I wasn't. I am rather alive. In fact, I think I am more alive than I have ever been."

Val looked at Elsinor confused. "Is he on medication?"

"Yes, a lot actually," Elsinor said. "But even if he were completely unmedicated I don't think we could get him to shut up about the woman who hit him."

"Oh? There is a woman involved? I should have known. Please tell me what planet does she call her own?" Comte Middleton said. "Is she human? AiJalonian? Engorian? Gadolan? Boy, stop me before I run out of species to zoom in."

"She is AiJalonian. Pure or nearly so. And she's beautiful," Maggie provided.

"Mahogany, go attend to your studies," Mrs. Dashing said.

"What? Why? I want to stay and talk of Madrick's new love!"

"Love?" Val asked. "It is love so soon then."

"It is as if I have been struck—"

"You have, you imbecile," Elsinor said, interrupting her brother. "I think you may want to wait until the swelling recedes before you declare your undying affection for a reckless driving mystery woman whom you may never see again."

"Oh, Elsinor, let him have his fantasies," Mrs. Dashing said. "Gaion knows we have little else."

An awkward pause fell over the room. Elsinor felt embarrassed for the words and behavior of her mother and brother. Sure, Madrick's fantasies were ridiculous and a bit embarrassing, but Elsinor was just having a little fun with him. Her mother pointing out that they had nothing was pouring salt into the open wound of their destitute and hopeless situation.

Madrick also felt the sting of his mother's remark and turned quiet and morose. Val suddenly felt as though she were intruding. Comte Middleton felt nothing but the overwhelming desire to know more about this mystery woman.

"Well, I come bearing gifts," Val said, breaking the somber silence. "When I heard that you injured your leg, I decided to help. I have with me the operating system for a medical droid as well as this," she said, handing him a cane. But not just any cane. It was her cane. "I am sure you won't need it for long. Once you have a droid that can examine you, I'm sure you'll only have a diagnosis of two to three weeks of invalidity, but I thought during that time, you could use some assistance."

"Thanks, Val. That is very kind of you." Madrick was genuinely touched. Most beings on AiJalon thought humans didn't deserve gifts. Given the fact that humans tried and failed to take over the planet when they first arrived, most thought it was a gift enough to just allow them to live. But here Val was providing gifts for them not once, but twice in a matter of weeks. "I don't understand though. Don't you need the cane?" he asked.

Val shook her head. "Not anymore." She lifted her leg and flexed her foot. "I took your advice and had my new leg attached last week. That is where I have been all this time. I am whole again."

Elsinor noticed another quiet stare between her brother and Val. There was definitely something between them and in her heart of hearts she really wanted them to explore that attraction. Unfortunately, she also felt that this new, recklessly driving mystery woman was about to complicate everyone's life somehow.

Elsinor half expected Madrick to reject assistance from Val. She thought he would be too proud to accept the operating system for the droid and the cane. But to her surprise, he not only accepted the gifts, but immediately began to upload the information into their servant droid. The Dashings were far too poor to own more than two droids so the droid they used for cleaning and cooking was also about to become the family doctor.

Madrick had the medical droid up and running within three minutes. With an entire operating system at his disposal, the modifications on the droid were quite simple ... for him at least.

As the droid examined Madrick, Val and Elsinor exited the room. Comte Middleton had already left with Maggie and Marzi in an attempt to find out more about the driver of the Earth vehicle.

"So, what do you know about this woman who hit him?" Val asked once they were outside. "Do you have her name?"

"Yes, it is Willow King."

Val's eyes expanded. "Willow King? Are you sure?"

"Yes, do you know her?" Elsinor asked, slightly intrigued by Val's reaction and facial expression. She truly seemed as though Elsinor had mentioned the name of a dead person.

"Yes. I know her well. But not as well as I thought. Obviously."

Elsinor wanted to ask what Val meant by this, but she heard her brother cry out in pain.

Running back inside, she said, "Maddie, what is happening?"

"Droid ... Batteries," was all he could manage to say.

Val knelt beside him and next to the droid. "This droid doesn't have enough energy to reset his bone properly. When is the last time he was charged?"

Madrick started screaming as the droid powered down while still clutching his leg.

"What do we do?" Elsinor asked.

"I'll take care of it." Val punched a few buttons on the droid and then pushed him aside. She then wrapped her hands around Madrick's leg before snapping the bone back in place with a sharp twist. Madrick passed out again from the pain. Looking through the perilously understocked medical kit that belonged to the Dashings, she mixed three chemicals together and then put the mixture into a syringe. After carefully injecting Madrick she said, "That should do it."

"What did you do? And more importantly, how did you learn to do it?" Elsinor asked.

Val shrugged. "Just something I picked up I guess."

"Picked up? Where? I've never met another AiJalonian that is so adept with medicine."

Before Val could answer, Madrick started regaining consciousness.

"What happened?" he asked.

"You passed out, but the droid was able to fix you up," Val offered as she gave Elsinor a look that said 'That is true enough.'

Elsinor was thoroughly confused. Not only was Val able to set Madrick's bone with her bare hands, but she had just told a lie about it with ease. But she was AiJalonian. How was that possible? Either Val was not pure AiJalonian or there was more to this woman than the Dashings knew.

# Chapter 18

The next morning, Willow dressed in her favorite sparkling blue handcrafted dressing gown. It was her absolute favorite not because she looked positively amazing in it or because it had cost her a near fortune to have it specially made. It was her favorite because she had expertly designed it to hold not one, not two, but three equalizers completely imperceptibly. Willow smiled, recalling a time on Lumerca when those compartments proved extremely useful. Lumercans were a bit more accustomed to violence than AiJalonians. Thus, when she was searched before entering a party, they found two of the equalizers, but not the third. And now, thankfully, due to that well-hidden compartment, there was a general there who would never be able to raise his hand to another woman, for he no longer had a hand. Those were two of the best shots she had ever taken. Imagine dancing in the middle of a ballroom and having both of your hands blown off

120

so precisely that nary a drop of blood splattered on an innocent person. It was an impossible shot. Two impossible shots. Legendary. Shots that only she, Willow King, could make with Gaion's help. She would be a legend one day. The subject of stories passed down from generation to generation. She should really consider choosing a moniker for herself. Maybe Weeping Willow. Eh, maybe not, she thought. That kind of made it seem like she was the one that cried. But that wasn't the case at all. She would never cry again.

Suddenly, she doubted her endeavor with Madrick. He was so handsome, and capable, and personable. He was like no one she had ever met. What if he made her cry? What if she truly fell for him so completely that she wouldn't be able to complete her mission as an Angel of Gaion?

Willow stood at the door of the Dashing domicilio holding her gifts. After careful research, she had determined that often courting rituals required gifts. She could not decide between flowers, Gadolan chocolate, and cinnamon wine so she brought all three. It never occurred to her to realize that suitors were most often men, but Willow had a way of seeing the world differently anyway.

There was a feeling in the bottom of her stomach. She wasn't quite sure what it was. It was similar to the feeling of excitement that filled her after ending the life of a being that no longer deserved to live. But this excitement was tinged with fear. Not the deadly fear she felt being held captive by a Harvothite, but a general fear of the future and the unknown. She could most closely relate this excitement tinged with fear that she felt with anxiety. She was anxious to see Madrick again but also anxious of what might come. All of these unfamiliar emotions lingered within her and made her want to dash back to her classic Mercedes and rush home. But she had just pushed the chime and the droid was already opening the door.

Willow was shown to the parlor which also served as the dining room and the sitting room in the miniscule domicilio where the Dashings resided. Their home was a fraction of the size of her own, but that didn't really bother her. One time on Tentor, Willow had to live for an entire month in something called a studio apartment while she stalked her prey. She adjusted quickly and by the end of the month, she'd kind of enjoyed it. Poverty didn't bother her. Of course, that was something she was rich enough to say.

Once in the parlor, her eyes moved from Mrs. Dashing to Elsinor to little Maggie. After giving them all a ceremonial bow, she found Madrick laying on a lounge. He was smiling. A smile so beautiful it almost instantly turned her into a weeping Willow. She had to remind herself that she was in control. This was a mission. She needed him to solve her equalizer problem and nothing more. But looking at him again, Willow knew she wanted more.

Everyone in the room stared at her oddly. No one spoke. It finally occurred to Willow that they were all probably wondering why she had come to their home.

Willow smiled. "I brought gifts for the invalid," she said cheerfully, extending them forward. It was not as smooth of an introduction as she had intended, but she was sure her confident smile made up for the insecurity she felt. "Flowers to fill the gloom, candy to sweeten his belly, and if all else fails, wine to numb the pain." That was better, she thought. The Willow charm she had been perfecting over the past three years was finally coming to the fore.

"Thank you," Elsinor said, taking them from her hand. "They are ... beautiful ... It was a beautiful thought.

"I felt I needed to return to once again convey my sincere apologies. I also wanted to make sure you are recovering, Madrick."

"I am. Thank you, Miss Willow." He was still smiling. Gaion, why was he doing that? Did he know what it did to her? For he undoubtedly had the most dashing smile on the planet. And his name was Dashing. It was as if Gaion knew what he would look like and thus ordained that he would have the appropriate name.

"May I offer you some tea?" Mrs. Dashing asked.

"Yes, tea. That may help," Willow said.

"Help with what?" Madrick asked. There was something in the tone of his voice that excited her. He was flirting again. He had said three simple words, but just the way he said them meant so much more. How did he do that? She was the one who was supposed to be pursuing him. But apparently, she had a lot to learn about courting. Willow needed to figure out a way to keep control.

"Elsinor, Maggie, I could use some assistance with the tea," Marzi said before exiting the room.

Maggie looked confused. "Since when does it take three people to make tea? A droid can do it in a matter of seconds."

"Mahogany Dashing, to the kitchen now."

Once the Dashing women had left the room, Willow took a seat near where Madrick lay. "Are you in pain? Has a medical droid examined you? Is there anything I can do to help?"

"Yes, yes, and you already are," he said, answering her three questions chronologically.

"I am what?"

"You are already helping me. You are my angel of Gaion. I feel no pain when you are near. So, yes, you are helping me."

Angel of Gaion. He had called her his angel of Gaion. It was a sign. Gaion wanted them to be together. For Willow already knew that she was Gaion's angel, exacting his punishment on the wicked. And for Madrick to use the same phrase, it was like Gaion telling her that he was the one. They were meant to be. Not only would he fix her equalizers, but he was the one that would finally fix her. He was the one that would fill the emptiness in her life. They could even complete her mission together.

Willow took a deep breath then said, "If you don't mind, and it is agreeable to you, I would like to enter into a mutual flirtation with you, Madrick Dashing." She didn't mean to come right out and say it like that. She had intended to handle the situation with a little more finesse. But it was as if the spirit of Gaion had filled her and moved her to speak those words.

His eyes widened.

"With me? Are you sure?" he asked.

"Absolutely," she said, touching his hand gently. "Why wouldn't I be?"

"Well, I am human. I look very AiJalonian, or so I have been told, but I am, indeed, half-human.

Are you sure your family would accept a flirtation with me? Have you asked their opinion?"

"I have no family. I am not dependent on anyone financially. So the only opinion that matters … is mine," she said with a shrug.

"And what exactly is your opinion of me?" he asked, caressing her hand in return.

"You are beautiful, talented and smart as evidenced by the fact that you fixed my car in mere moments." Willow smiled then added, "And you evidently have a very high pain tolerance which can be exceedingly beneficial in certain circumstances."

Madrick looked confused.

"High pain tolerance?" he asked. "Is it your intent to cause me pain, Willow King?"

"It is my intent for us to enjoy all the peace and happiness that is in Gaion's power to give." At this point, Willow badly wanted to kiss him. She had never had a real kiss, only those done in deception to lure in a mark. She had never kissed a man because of her own desire. She deeply desired Madrick. More than she wanted to admit. But it would be highly inappropriate to perform such an intimate act just one day after meeting and mere seconds after beginning a flirtation. Suddenly, she remembered that he never actually agreed to the flirtation. "That is, if you are so inclined to enter into a mutual flirtation with me."

Madrick reached up his hand and caressed her cheek then gently ran his thumb across her bottom lip. Willow's heart nearly burst out of her chest. If just his thumb on her lip could cause her body to erupt in such delight, she wondered what his lips could do.

"Willow King, nothing on the planet would please me more."

# Chapter 19

"And just what makes you think I can fix an equalizer?" Madrick asked one afternoon as he and Willow were sitting by a lake. She had to force herself to remember to even bring up the topic of equalizers. It had been two weeks since they had entered into their mutual flirtation and Willow had found that every time she was near him, thoughts of equalizers and Gaion's mission just floated out of her mind. All she cared about recently was being near him. That had to change.

Willow didn't know what was happening to her. She couldn't explain the emotions she felt when she was around Madrick. When he was near, it was like she was floating. When he was away, there was a pain in her heart. She had recorded him playing a song on the bandalore and found that at night, when she was alone, it brought her great comfort to hear it over and over again. When she closed her eyes, images of his smile brought her great pleasure. Oh, why was she lying to herself? She knew exactly what was happening ... well what had already happened. She, Willow King, was in love. That thought terrified her. The last time she thought she was in love, she'd ended up in a paedor as a slave.

It was a terrifying realization. In certain situations, loving another person could be extremely dangerous. What if she had to choose between her love for Madrick and her love for Gaion? What would she choose? But on the other hand, this emotion could also be very useful. She often had to feign emotions in order to lure in her targets. Now that she had actually felt this emotion called love, perhaps she would be even better at pretending.

"Willow?" Madrick asked when she didn't respond. "I said, what makes you think I can fix an equalizer?"

"You are a genius, Madrick Dashing. And don't even pretend you don't know it. You can fix anything."

Madrick turned the equalizer around in his hand. "Why do you even have this?"

Willow had considered how she would answer this question. She thought she had built up the courage to tell him the truth. To tell him that she was on a mission from Gaion and that she wanted him to join her. But now, sitting next to this lake whose beauty only paled in Madrick's presence, she found she couldn't do it. What if he rejected her? She couldn't risk losing him. Not yet. Not when she was currently the happiest she had ever been in her life. Willow needed to answer the question in a way that wasn't a lie but not completely the truth.

"I find them fascinating," Willow said finally. "Much like Earth cars. A relic of the past."

Thankfully, that answer satisfied him for the moment. He seemed engrossed in the mechanics of the equalizer and had probably already worked out three ways to fix it. Willow knew she had made the right decision in asking him for help. They would make a great team. She could train him and teach him to fight just as Val had done with her.

Thinking of Val, Willow had noticed something strange in her former mentor. Over the past two weeks, Willow saw how Val looked at Madrick. It was the same way she used to look at Milo. It was obvious to her that Val was also in love with Madrick as well. Poor Val. First to lose Milo so horrifically and right in front of her and then to not be able to have the love of Madrick. For Madrick belonged to Willow. Heart, mind and soul. He adored her as much as she adored him. She knew it. And she would never let him go. Not willingly anyway.

"What are you thinking about?" Madrick asked several minutes later. He set down the equalizer, picked up his bandalore and began strumming a loving ballad.

Snapping out of her reverie, Willow looked upon his face. It was perfection in a moment. "You," she answered honestly. "I'm thinking about you."

"Is that right?" Madrick set down the instrument and scooted closer to Willow. "And what exactly about me has captured your thoughts?" He was now so close to her that their noses almost touched. "Is it the way my fingers strum the bandalore?" he asked as he gently brushed his fingers up the side of her arm.

A tingling sensation erupted all over Willow's body.

"Or is it the way my lips involuntarily draw into a smile whenever you are around?" Without waiting for her to respond, Madrick leaned in and caressed her lips with his own.

Willow searched her emotions. What was this feeling of Madrick's lips on hers? She could barely describe it. She could barely think. All she knew was that she absolutely did not want it to end.

So, this was kissing. Real kissing. Not merely pressing her lips to a man in order to convince him to follow her to his death. This was passion. This was what was so popular among other cultures like the humans and Engorians. It wasn't something

131

AiJalonians did too often, not until other species introduced it. Willow suddenly felt sorry for every AiJalonian who never got to experience this. For if they ever had the opportunity to kiss someone even half as skilled in the art as Madrick, they could consider themselves extremely blessed by Gaion.

Madrick pressed himself against her as he gently lowered her onto the grass. Their bodies felt as though they were molding into one. Then suddenly, images of the Harvothite that had held her captive in the paedor arose in her mind. Thoughts of what he was training her to do once she was given over to her master on Olevia.

She pushed Madrick away.

"Stop. Just stop!" she said.

"I'm sorry. Am I moving too fast?" he asked, truly concerned by her reaction to his advances.

"No ... Yes ... No. I want to ... with you. But, I can't. I just can't."

Turning away, Willow brought her legs to her chest and curled herself into a tight ball. She wanted to block out the world. She knew she had probably completely confused him, but in that moment, she didn't care. She didn't want to be touched. She couldn't be touched. She expected Madrick to realize this and leave her alone, perhaps forever. She didn't want him to go away forever. She wanted him to be a part of her life. But she suddenly had the realization that that might never be possible. Maybe she was incapable of love. Having a healthy, loving relationship might not be in Gaion's plan for her after all.

"Willow," Madrick said moments later. He was still there. He hadn't left. "Are you okay?"

She shook her head. "No, I'm not. And I might not ever be."

"Whatever it is, we can figure it out together. You don't have to be alone. Just talk to me." He reached out to touch her and she scooted away further.

***

The next thing she remembered, she turned around and Madrick was gone. She didn't know how long she had stayed there huddled into a ball, trying to make herself as little and insignificant as possible. She wondered how long Madrick had stayed with her before he had finally taken her request to be alone seriously and left. Part of her hoped that Madrick had left forever. She was no good for him. She was too damaged to ever be the loving mate he deserved.

As Willow stood to return home, she felt as if she were being watched. Could the intergalactic police finally have caught up with her? She knew she should have left the planet completely for a while after killing Senator Provem. The only reason she had stayed was because of Madrick. Now she had probably successfully scared him away. Willow pulled out an equalizer from one of her gown compartments. It didn't work anymore, but hopefully her assailant wouldn't realize it.

"Put down your weapon, it's me," Val said, stepping out from the trees and onto the shore of the lake.

"Val," Willow said, returning her equalizer to the fold of her skirt. "I was wondering how long it would take for you to seek me out." Willow actually felt comfortable with this line of communication. She thrived on confrontation. And no doubt Val wanted to discuss Willow's calling from Gaion. Val was not a true believer and would most likely try to talk her out of her mission.

"Why are you here, Willow?"

"Where? By the lake?"

"In Haran."

"Ah, well you should specify," Willow said with a grin.

"Would you like for me to permanently wipe that grin off your face?" Val asked.

"I would like to see you try," she responded.

Val sighed. "I don't want to fight with you. I simply want to know what your intentions are with Madrick."

"Madrick? What concern is Madrick Dashing to you? Is he your relation?"

"He is of no special concern to me. I just don't want to see him ... dragged into your kind of crazy. He doesn't deserve that."

Willow could not dispute this since she was actually just thinking the exact same thing.

"He is part-human. You have to remember he feels his emotions much more strongly than you or I. How is he going to feel when he finds out what you really are?"

Willow's eyes expanded in anger. "What do you mean WHAT I really am? Are you calling me a paedor slave?"

"No, Willow, of course not. You are not a paedor slave. What happened to you was against your will and is in no way your fault. But what you have become since, is."

"What are you trying to say?"

"I am not TRYING to say anything. I am declaratively stating that you are a murderer."

Willow rolled her eyes and scoffed. "That term does not apply to me as I only exterminate people who deserve it."

"I don't want to argue semantics with you. I am just here to tell you that if you do not plan on giving up this life you lead, then you need to give up Madrick. Immediately."

"What if he wants to live this life with me?"

"If you thought that was even in the remotest of possibilities, you would have told him who you are by now."

Willow couldn't argue with this either. Instead, she decided to redirect the conversation. "And what about you? Have you told him who you really are? What you really do?"

"That is not of his concern as we are not in a mutual flirtation. You and he are, thus, he deserves to know."

Once again, Val had a valid point, but Willow was in no way about to own to it. Emotions that Willow did not like began to rise. So in order to hold them down, she went on the offense. "And what do you plan on doing if I don't? Are you going to reveal the truth for me?"

"That is not my place. But just know, I will do what I have to do to make sure Madrick Dashing does not get hurt." With that, Val turned around and left the shore, leaving Willow with the beginnings of a plan.

# Chapter 20

Days later, the familiar sound of a duster broke the morning silence at Barton Domicilio. Elsinor and Maggie looked at Madrick.

"Why are you all looking at me?"

"Well, you are the only one at Barton who could possibly be riding a duster," Maggie said.

"In all of Haran actually," Elsinor added.

"As if I could be riding a duster and sitting in this room at the same time," he said.

"Valid argument," Marzi Dashing said as she approached the window to look out.

"Oh, my. Is that ... ?" Mrs. Dashing paused as if she was afraid of saying something incorrect.

Mahogany stood and looked out of the window next to her mother. "It's Edgar! It's Edgar!" she cried as she dashed out of the door to greet him.

"Edgar, you've come! You've finally come!" Elsinor could hear her sister greeting Edgar. She heard the sound of his duster whir to a stop, yet she didn't move.

Madrick placed his hand over his sister's. "You all right?"

"Yes, quite," she assured him. But in all honesty, she was not.

The little lie was enough assurance for Madrick, however, as he immediately went outside to greet his friend.

By the time Elsinor had composed herself enough to join the party outside, Madrick and Edgar were already discussing his duster.

*\*\**

When Elsinor appeared in the doorway, all thoughts of dusters left Edgar's mind. All at once he knew that coming to Barton Domicilio was both the dumbest decision he had ever made and the only one that could keep him breathing. Elsinor was just as beautiful as the last time he had seen her. More so. Somehow the month apart from her had made her more beautiful. Was that even possible? Judging from the tightening he felt in his chest, he knew that it was.

"You must stay for dinner," Mrs. Dashing said as she gestured for him to enter the domicilio.

"I can only stay for a few hours," Edgar said, not taking his eyes off of Elsinor.

"A few hours?" Maggie whined. "Why not longer? You could stay a week. Madrick wouldn't mind sharing a room with you."

"I really wouldn't mind at all," Madrick said. "I've missed you, Eddie. You are like the brother I never had."

"I am honored at the invitation," Edgar said. "I never feel so much a part of a family as I do when I am with you all."

"Then it's settled!" Madrick said. "You will stay the week."

"No, honestly, I cannot. I have already been away from Cosmo for a week; I must get back." The silence bespoke the disappointment of all. "I was in Plyon, you see, visiting some old acquaintance," Edgar added by way of explanation.

"Well, if we only have you for the day, we must make the best of it then," Madrick said.

"Madrick," Mrs. Dashing said. "Don't monopolize Edgar. I am sure he wants to spend some time with Elsinor."

All of the Dashings stared at him, expecting him to agree with this statement. Of course, it was true. He had come to spend time with Elsinor, which was the biggest reason why it was the completely inappropriate thing to do. He was not in a position to make such statements in public. "I have come to spend time with all of you," Edgar said finally.

After an early dinner, the Dashings and Edgar took a stroll around Haran.

Madrick, Mahogany and Marzi made a pointed effort to walk briskly, allowing Edgar and Elsinor to lag behind.

"As you can see," Elsinor said, "there is perhaps less to see here in Haran than there was in Castille."

"Well, you are close enough to the sea," Edgar said. "Have you made any new sea friends?"

Elsinor nodded. "I have befriended several schools of flicker fish, a very wise sea turtle, and a few landerbins, but I have yet to find Lutus again."

"Oh, I am sorry to hear that."

"It is okay," she said. "Sometimes beings are merely meant to be in your life for a moment. And then it is time to move on."

Edgar did not like the truth in her words.


"You know you are always welcome to stay as long as you like," Elsinor said moments later.

"And if it were my choice I would perhaps stay forever. But it is not."

"What do you mean?" she asked. "You are a young, single AiJalonian man of great fortune. You can choose to do anything you want."

"I wish it were so."

Elsinor sighed. "I know what you mean."

He stopped walking. "You do?"

Nodding, she said, "Of course I do. I know what you mean probably better than anyone ever could. Do you forget that I am half-human? I am a mistura. I have very little choice in anything that I do. I am restricted in where I live, what I can own and if I visit Cosmo, I am even restricted in what I can wear. And I have absolutely no choice in the matter. It may seem as though I am accepting of the situation. That I bear my lack of choice with aplomb. But inside I suffer as I am sure you are suffering inside right now."

"What helps you to bear it as you say?" he asked, genuinely curious as to how her family tolerated the treatment of humans. What he suffered was nothing in comparison. If he knew her secret, maybe it would help him as well.

Elsinor shrugged. "I suppose it is faith in the idea that one day everything will be as it should."

Edgar wished he had that kind of faith.

All too soon his visit ended.

"Don't be so morose, friend," Madrick said. "We will see each other again soon."

Edgar too felt they would see each other again soon, but he wasn't so sure it would be a happy occasion.

"So did he ask you?" Madrick asked as Edgar rode off into the night.

"Ask me what?" Elsinor responded.

"Well, to marry you of course. Am I to have a brother at long last?"

"No," she said simply.

"No? He didn't propose marriage? Why on AiJalon did he come here then?"

"I have no idea."

# Chapter 21

Regular summits were something that happened on most islands and archipelagos on AiJalon. Even pure AiJalonian families who suffered no admixture from other species for generations had been influenced enough by other cultures to require the revelry of summits. It gave the young people an opportunity to meet each other and fall in love on their own instead of being matched by their parents and trapped in an arranged marriage. Of course, there were not island style summits in Cosmo which was still heavily influenced by traditional AiJalonian values of purity and logic. The AiJalonian Ministry of Purity deemed it completely illogical that one could find a lifelong mate by chance at something as frivolous as a dance like a summit. Thus, they were held completely differently and highly regulated within the city limits of Cosmo.

Comtesa Middleton always regretted not attending summits when she was young and of marrying age. Maybe then she could have avoided this tragic marriage she found herself in to the Comte. It was probably because of this that she loved to hold her own summits in her home. Unfortunately, the Middletons lived in Haran. It was nearly a desolate island where there were hardly enough opportunities to hold one as there were not nearly enough people. So, with the Dashings living in their domicilio and her cousins the Satterlys visiting, she felt it was definitely time to hold one at Barton Hall.

After a few days of planning, she had gathered enough people to visit from out of town in order to hold a valid party.

"Gaion! Cai'ana, why are you doing this?" Val asked her friend as they prepared for the party.

"I will not permit you to whine about my summit, Val. It is an opportunity to meet people. To fall in love truly, not artificially which is the AiJalonian way," her friend responded. "Besides, I am doing this for you as well. Since you won't admit that you have feelings for Madrick—"

"I do not ..." Val began in protest but found she was unable to finish her thought in truth.

"Well, he certainly stirs my feelings. That much is certain," Cai said. "I'm married, so I can say this. That boy is the most exquisitely handsome creature I have ever laid eyes on in my life."

"I pretty sure being married is precisely why you CANNOT say that."

"Whatever. Look, all I am saying, is that as a living, breathing woman with eyes, there is no possible way you haven't noticed his beauty. I swear to Gaion, every time I see him, I have to let out a string of Minnithite profanities in my mind."

"They do have the most descriptive profanities," Val admitted.

"Yes, exactly! In what other language can you find one word to say that someone is so physically perfect you would birth a thousand of their children? *Dishevecik.*"

"Cai, a little decency please."

"Anyway," Cai continued, "since you won't admit that Madrick is simply a god in half-human, half-AiJalonian form, perhaps there will be another young man there who meets your fancy."

"I'm too old to meet someone."

"Say something that stupid again and I swear to Gaion I will chug a bottle of Gadolan liquor."

Val sighed and rolled her eyes, a very human habit she had picked up from her friend Elloree Darkeny.

"I'm serious. I have a bottle in my drawer right here." Cai'ana continued, "You are only twenty and four. If you're old, I'm knocking on death's door."

"First of all, I'm only twenty-three. Second, you realize you rhymed right?"

145

"Humph. I did. Well, rules are rules." Cai'ana opened her drawer and pulled out the bottle of Sweet Gadolan rum.

"What rules?" Val asked, snatching the bottle away. "You are not making any sense. I thought you drank when your husband rhymed. You can't just make a rhyme yourself and then drink to it. You just want an excuse to retreat into your alcohol and not deal with your life."

"Have you seen my life?" Cai'ana said. "You would drink too if you had to live like this. Plus, my sister is coming. You know how she drives me crazy."

"Everyone drives you crazy lately, Cai. What is this really about?"

Cai'ana sat down on the bed. "I am so unhappy."

"Yes, I gathered that. But why?"

"Why?" Cai'ana said in astonishment. "You see my life. I am married to a ridiculous man who doesn't speak unless it is to rhyme."

"You did not have to marry him. Many people reject arranged marriages."

"Of course I did. It is the AiJalonian way. I didn't know I had another option. Not until I met you. I am so jealous of your life sometimes. You seem so free."

Val sat down on the bed. "Cai, you really have no need to be jealous of me. My life ... my life is not

146

some sort of adventurous fairy tale no matter how many space odyssey novels you read."

Val and Cai sat in silence for a moment. "If she hadn't disappeared the way she did," Cai'ana said finally, "I might have chosen differently."

Even without saying the name specifically, Val knew Cai was speaking of her sister. Dahlonega Greer and Cai'ana had been best friends. When she disappeared, both of their lives changed forever, just in different ways.

"I was afraid," Cai'ana said. "I was afraid the same thing could happen to me and I could end up in a—" She couldn't bring herself to say the word.

Even though there was no actual proof that Val's sister had ended up a paedor slave, it was a safe assumption given what Val had learned about the trafficking trade.

"In any case," she continued, "I accepted the first marriage mate arranged for me. I hadn't said more than three words to J'ao. And now I am stuck forever. Meanwhile, you did the opposite. You saw an injustice and dedicated your life to making it right."

"And what good has it done me? I lost not only my sister, but the man I loved."

"How did it happen?" Cai'ana asked her friend.

Val closed her eyes and shook her head. She was not ready to talk about Milo's death. She wasn't sure she would ever be ready.

***

Val was also not quite ready to admit to herself, let alone Cai'ana, that she had feelings for Madrick Dashing. Even if she could admit it, it wouldn't have done any good. He was completely and utterly enamored with Willow King. She considered the idea of pulling him aside and telling him the kind of person Willow was. Telling him that she was a psychotic murderer who had the blood of several men on her hands. But what would that have accomplished? Besides, he looked so happy. And so did she for that matter. Who was she to impose upon their happiness? Maybe they belonged together. Maybe he would be the calming effect she needed in her life.

Val shook her head. It didn't matter. Madrick didn't look twice at her whenever Willow was in the room. She had lost him and had no hope of ever gaining his love.

She had half a mind to go back up to Cai'ana's room and open that bottle of sweet Gadolan rum. She surely didn't want to stand around and watch Willow and Madrick dance anymore. Val was about to turn and head upstairs in search of the rum when both Willow and Madrick approached her.

"Val, have you met Willow?" Madrick asked.

"Actually, I have." The fact that he didn't know that she and Willow already knew each other told her everything she needed to know. Willow had no intention of telling Madrick the truth about her past.

"Why are you not dancing?" Willow asked artfully. She was diverting the conversation away from their shared history.

"There seems to be a shortage of young men," Val said diplomatically. The truth was all the young men were interested in women that were younger than her. Unfortunately, in AiJalonian culture, if you were not married by twenty years of age, you were virtually an old maid spinster.

"Maddie, why don't you dance with her?" Willow asked, offering up Madrick as if he was her special property.

Val should have been offended at Willow's power move. But seeing the smile on Madrick's face, somehow she was not. She wanted nothing more than to have just a few minutes in his arms.

"What do you say, Val? Shall we dance?" As Madrick took her hand in his, she felt tingles shoot up her arm and into her chest. She took a deep breath to calm herself. There was no denying. She was in love with this man. It was absurd, but it didn't change the fact that one simple touch from him sent her heart aflutter. *Dishevecik*, she thought.

Madrick led her to the dance floor to wait for the next song to begin. It was during this time that her personal receiver chimed. She thought about ignoring it, but for someone with her past, ignoring a TelEx could mean death, perhaps for someone she cared about. She needed to take a quick peek at the sender and then decide if she could wait to answer it after the dance or not. After she saw FontL'Roy Darkeny's image on her receiver, she knew it could not be delayed even for a second. FontL'Roy knew how she was taking some much needed time for herself so if he was trying to contact her, it had to be of the utmost importance.

"I'm sorry," Val said to Madrick. "I have to go."

"But we haven't danced yet."

"I know and I'm sorry, but it is an emergency."

"What's wrong?" Willow said, joining them.

Not wanting to let Willow know she had gotten a message from FontL'Roy, she simply said, "I am not feeling well and I will not be able to dance with Madrick. Surely you will not mind dancing in my place."

"Not at all," Willow said, placing a possessive arm around Madrick.

Val felt an emptiness in her heart. This was perhaps her one and only chance to have an intimate moment with Madrick. But it could not be avoided. If Font or his wife were in trouble, she'd never forgive herself. "You must excuse me."

Val ran upstairs and took out her TelEx to listen to the message from her friend Font.

"Val, I hope this message reaches you in good health. I am writing because I need your help. Please respond immediately if you are available for an assist."

Truth be told, Val was more than happy for the distraction of assisting Font on a mission. For personal and emotional reasons, she had extricated herself from the entire mission situation. FontL'Roy and his wife were completely capable of any mission that could possibly come their way so she was slightly curious as to why they needed her, but she didn't ask questions. She sent a quick response that she was on her way and then changed into more appropriate clothing: tan pants and a dark vest that included an equalizer holder.

## Chapter 22

Elsinor watched hopefully as her brother escorted Val to the dance floor. Maybe this was the setting they needed. Maybe a romantic jaunt about the dance floor would be enough to loosen Willow's hold on Madrick and make him realize that Val was the one he needed. Unfortunately, that was not what happened. Before the music even started, Val excused herself and ran upstairs. Elsinor was just about to follow and inquire after her when three women stepped in her path.

"You must be Elsinor Dashing," the older of the three said.

"Yes, I am."

"Oh, it is so nice to meet you! I am Chai'loi Palmer. I'm sure you have heard all about me from my older sister Cai'ana."

Chai'loi stared at Elsinor, apparently awaiting an affirmative response. The truth was, Elsinor could not remember Comtesa Middleton mentioning her sister at all. She did remember Mrs. Jensent saying something about her on their first day so she was able to say, "Indeed, your name has been mentioned."

"Yes, my sister is remarkably attached to me. We are best friends and I look up to her so much."

"Ah," was all Elsinor could manage to say. Honestly, she could not imagine Comtesa Middleton being remarkably attached to anything besides a liquor bottle.

"Do let me introduce my cousins, Lace and Anna," Chai'loi said. "Mr. Palmer and I picked them up in Plyon on our way here and I daresay that they could not stop talking of you, Miss Dashing."

"Me? But why would—?"

"Oh, it is so good to meet you," one of the girls said, not allowing time for Elsinor to finish her question. "I have heard oh so much about you."

"Yes, I have just been told. But may I ask from whom?"

"From an acquaintance we share," she said.

"An acquaintance—"

"And this is my sister," the woman said of the other young lady, once again interrupting Elsinor.

"Oh, look. There is Cai'ana," Chai'loi said, waving across the room. "Cai, Cai it's me. Look how excited she is to see me." Elsinor turned just in time to see Comtesa Middleton pour herself a glass of wine. She closed her eyes, took a sip, and then smiled at her sister. Elsinor couldn't help but think that the comtesa said a brief prayer to Gaion asking for strength.

"And there," Chai'loi continued. "There. Right there is my handsome husband Mr. Palmer."

The man who Elsinor assumed was Mr. Palmer deftly ducked into a hallway and avoided eye contact with his wife. In just a matter of moments, Elsinor had surmised that many people probably tried to avoid contact with Chai'loi. "Oh, bother, he must have gotten an important TelEx from Cosmo that he needs to answer. He has such an important job we rarely get to get away to the islands like this. Oh, I do hope he is not called back to the capital. We only just arrived here. I'll just go inquire about the matter."

Elsinor was unable to comment on the line of reasoning as she was too amazed at how Chai'loi seemed to say all of it on one single breath. Suddenly, she understood the common nickname Chatty Chai'.

"Is this her?" the second sister asked once Chai'loi dashed away to see her husband.

"Yes, it is," the first sister said.

"Oh, how exciting. Have you told her all?"

"I've told her nothing. We only just met."

"Oh but you will tell her, won't you? You will tell her all."

"Well, of course I will. That is the whole point, is it not?"

The two women spoke so quickly it was as if they didn't need time to draw breath. Elsinor's head just bobbed back and forth between them as if she was following a ball back and forth across the net in a game of Volenstick.

"Sorry, please," Elsinor said finally interrupting them. "Who are you?"

The girls giggled. "So sorry. We tend to get carried away when we are excited. And we are oh so excited to meet you. But my name is Lace. Lace Satterly and this is my sister Anna."

"Satterly, yes," Elsinor said. "You are the Middletons' cousins from Plyon."

Lace and Anna each took one of Elsinor's arms and walked with her around and around the ballroom as they chatted incessantly.

"So what do you think?" Lace asked.

"Excuse me?" Elsinor realized that she hadn't been paying any attention to the conversation. In fact, most of the time she had no idea if either of them were directly speaking to her or not.

"Anna went off for a dance. What do you think about the two of us taking a stroll down to the lake?" Lace asked again.

Elsinor had to admit that it sounded like a good idea. She hadn't been to a lake in a few days. When she first arrived in Haran, she made it a point to visit a lake at least once a day. It gave her time to meditate on Gaion's creation as well as to think about Edgar.

Every time she sat on the shore of a lake and dipped her feet into the shimmering water, she liked to imagine that he was somewhere on AiJalon doing the same.

"That sounds like an excellent idea."

"I have to say," Lace said as they were walking, "I am so happy to finally get you alone."

"Excuse me?" Elsinor asked, confused. What on AiJalon did that mean? Did this girl have some sort of weird obsession with her?

"Yes, I have heard so much about you, I know I can trust your opinion," she said. "I am in quite a difficult situation."

"Oh, I am sorry to hear that," Elsinor said, relieved that she was wrong about the obsession assumption. She wasn't exactly interested in what Lace's problem actually was and she felt bad about that. She was going to try to pay more attention. "What seems to be your difficult situation?" Elsinor asked, doing her best to feign genuine concern.

"Do you know much about your half-brother's mother-in-law?"

"Mrs. Fyatt? No, I have never met her."

"Have you heard as to whether she is agreeable or not? Dear Gaion, I do hope that she is."

"May I ask why you are concerned about the personality traits of my half-brother's mother-in-law?"

Lace giggled. "Oh, I apologize. You must think me very odd indeed. I guess I should tell you the whole truth, but you must promise not to tell a soul. It is a very massive secret."

"If it is such an important secret perhaps you should not reveal it to me. We are only of short acquaintance."

"But you see, I must tell someone for fear it will eat me alive."

Lace seemed extremely desperate to tell her secret and Elsinor hated to see anyone uncomfortable. For this reason alone she agreed to keep the information confidential.

"The reason I am so interested in your half-brother's mother-in-law is because some day she will be my mother-in-law as well."

Elsinor stopped walking for a moment and tried to work through this information in her head. The only other brother besides Edgar that Femili had was Roymond. Was Lace engaged to Roymond Fyatt? How would they have even met?

"Do you have an arrangement with Roymond Fyatt?" Elsinor asked.

"Oh no, not Roymond. I have never met him before in my life. I am engaged to his brother, Edgar."

Elsinor suddenly felt short of breath. "Edgar Fyatt? You are engaged to Edgar Fyatt?"

"Yes, I am. I love him so. And he loves me too."

"Edgar Fyatt of Cosmo?"

"Yes, the one and only."

The ground felt as though it was swirling beneath her. Elsinor reached for a tree and leaned against it for fear that otherwise she would collapse to the ground.

"And may I ask," she began. She paused for a second in order to make sure her voice remained steady. "May I ask how long you have been in this engagement?"

"Four years," Lace said. "We met four years ago in Plyon where Edgar went to school."

"Plyon," Elsinor repeated. Immediately, in her mind she heard that word spoken in Edgar's voice. She remembered him talking about it. He had tried to tell her something. Then suddenly, it all made sense. He always seemed like he had something to say to her but couldn't. And this was it. His actions, his looks, even the brushes of his hand when they accidentally touched hers, everything pointed to the fact that he loved her, but he wasn't at liberty to say such a thing. Not when he was in a long-standing relationship with another woman.

Immediately, her heart ached for Edgar. Partly because she knew she could never have him for herself, but also because she felt his pain. How difficult those weeks at Nova must have been for him! She knew how he really felt. Anyone who looked in his eyes could know what he really felt for her. That was why Femili was so determined to get him to leave. She didn't want them together any longer than necessary so their attachment wouldn't get any stronger. To have all of this weighing on him. No wonder he stuttered.

Did he still love Lace? Had he ever loved Lace? It didn't really matter. He had made a promise to her and if Elsinor knew anything about him, she knew he would keep that promise no matter what it meant to his own personal feelings.

"Are you all right, Elsinor?"

Elsinor realized that she hadn't said anything in several minutes and that she was still holding on to the tree. She needed to compose herself.

"Yes, I'm fine."

"I know it must be quite a shock for you. Though I am surprised he did not mention me or at least Plyon."

"He mentioned Plyon," Elsinor said, remembering that last conversation they had.

"Ah, I thought he might. He was so enamored with the entire region I am sure he mentions it quite often. Though his adoration of the island may have more to do with me than with the actual location." Lace attempted a demure smile, but Elsinor noted there was a touch of boastfulness in it. "He has visited me since visiting Nova and he mentioned you. He mentioned you by name actually."

"Did he?" Elsinor asked, genuinely intrigued.

159

"Oh yes, he mentioned that he truly treasured your FRIENDSHIP and that he thought of you as a SISTER he never had." Lace made special effort to emphasize the words 'friendship' and 'sister' and Elsinor knew exactly why. Jealousy was not a common emotion among AiJalonian people. In fact, it was one of the least prevalent in most cases. Jealousy was not a logical emotion. And in this case, it was rather illogical for Lace to be jealous of Elsinor. Lace was the one who had Edgar's promise. An engagement was as binding as a marriage. By law, an engaged couple were emotionally married. The forthcoming marriage ceremony only served to bind them publicly and physically. So, for all intents and purposes, Lace was already Edgar's bride. But for some reason, Lace still felt threatened enough by Elsinor to find the need to put her in her place. She needed to remind Elsinor that she would never be more than a friend or 'sister' to him.

The point was received in full by Elsinor. She knew exactly where she stood.

\*\*\*

"Well, that Lace Satterly is a bit of a Chatty Chai', is she not?" Madrick asked when they had returned to the domicilio.

"Yes, I suppose."

"What did she bend your ear about all evening?"

Elsinor so wanted to confide in her brother. Maybe he could offer her some semblance of comfort. But she was sworn to secrecy. Besides, deep down she knew there was nothing that would be able to comfort her anyway. She was doomed to bear this agony alone.

"Nothing of consequence," she said finally.

"Did you notice how suddenly Val left this evening?"

"Yes, yes I did," Elsinor said, happy to be speaking on a topic other than Lace Satterly. "I hope everything is okay."

"And I hope I did not do something to offend her."

"Why do you say that?"

Madrick shrugged then took a seat on the lounge. "I don't know. I thought she would want to dance with me, but then almost as soon as I touched her, she made some excuse and ran away. It was as if I repulsed her or something."

"I am sure that is not the case," Elsinor said, sitting near the window. "If Val left suddenly, I am sure it was because of something very important." After staring out of the window at the evening sky, a thought popped into her head. "Since when do you care if Val finds you repulsive or not?" she asked.

Madrick hopped up from his seat with a frustrated flounce. "Gaion, Elsie. Why do you have to read into everything?" he asked before storming out of the room.

"Maddie, what did I say?"

# Chapter 23

"What is the plan, Font?" Val asked into the holotransmitter.

"And hello to you, too," FontL'Roy Darkeny responded.

"I'm sorry," she said. "I'm a little distracted. Your message caught me off guard. How is Elloree?"

"Pregnant," Darkeny said simply.

"Oh. Oh! Congratulations," she said. "Font, I am so happy for you. I now understand why you need me. A battle in a paedor is no place for a pregnant woman."

"Yes," was his only response.

"But you could have called Clintok or Barvery. They are very trained and much closer to Paedor III than I am here in Haran. Were they not available?"

After taking a deep breath, FontL'Roy said, "We will discuss that later." That was the best FontL'Roy could do at lying. Because of their extremely logical dispositions, all AiJalonians had difficulty telling falsehoods. FontL'Roy was one of the worst at it. Lying made him physically ill. Of course, there were different techniques to overcome this that Val had taught him, but of all the training, that was the one aspect where he did not excel.

Val stared at his hologram skeptically. He seemed to be hiding something. Was there another reason he needed her specifically for this mission? He knew very well that Val had decided to take a year or two off from their work. It was an extremely difficult decision, but there were a number of factors that made it obvious that it was the right thing to do. Her own mental health was at stake.

She didn't leave the cause lightly. Val had spent over a year training FontL'Roy and Elloree as her replacements. She had also had a team of six well-trained associates that they could call on for help instantly.

"Font, speak plainly," Val said. "Why did you call me?"

FontL'Roy sighed. "Leaven CoZark."

Val clicked off the holo and stopped her guster. She needed to get control of her emotions. She didn't know the exact situation. She didn't know whether CoZark was dead, alive or captured. But anything having to do with that man was enough to spark unmitigated rage within her spirit.

Leaven CoZark was a ruthless slave trader known for abusing his purchases so markedly that their bodies and spirits gave out within a few months.

Though she never had any proof, Val had reason to believe that he had something to do with her sister's disappearance thirteen years ago. When she was just ten years old and her sister seventeen, Leaven CoZark had a business meeting with their father. Even at that young age, Val recognized that CoZark looked at her sister oddly. She didn't like being around him and she tried to tell that to her parents but children were not often listened to. Shortly thereafter, her sister disappeared.

As Val began the search for her sister, she learned about the slave trade that secretly plagued AiJalon. She hoped that her sister had merely run away and had not been kidnapped and sold. But as Val learned more about the dark dealings that went down in the paedors, she learned of Cozark's connection to it. And his name kept coming up again and again. Val became convinced that he was the one who had taken her sister, but she didn't have any proof.

For thirteen years, she had chased the shadowy man with no success. Then, about a year and a half ago, she had a direct encounter with him.

She had followed him to a bar in Paedor IV. She stared at him as he drank drink after drink and laughed and joked with his friends. She was paralyzed. So many thoughts ran through her mind. The ideas of what he had probably done with so many girls including her sister. It was unacceptable. She reached for her equalizer, aimed and fired. Nothing happened. She had stared at him so long that she lost all track of time and did not realize that the core had shifted rendering her weapon useless. She threw down the equalizer and ran out of the establishment, completely horrified at what she was about to do.

She was about to murder a man in public with no evidence at all of his wrongdoing. Not only that, but if he was the one to take her sister, killing him was not the way to find out more information about her whereabouts.

Val realized then that something was wrong. She was not in her right mind. Perhaps the combined weight of losing her sister, Milo and her leg was too much to bear. That's when she decided to leave the battle for a little while. She returned to AiJalon proper and began to visit some of her old friends, especially ones that knew her sister. She needed calm and stability. She needed to remember what her mission was. She needed to not become a Willow King.

After taking several deep calming breaths, she turned her holo back on.

"Are you still there, Font?"

"I am. How are you?" he asked.

"I'm fine."

"Are you sure? I can call Clintok or Barvery if you are not up for this."

"I'm fine. What do we know?"

"CoZark made a mistake," Font said. "An expired plate on his guster precipitated a search of it from the intergalactic police. Everything on his guster was registered, including a minute amount of blood that matched ... The DNA was a confirmed match ... "

"Spit it out, Font!"

"Dahlonega. The blood came from your sister, Dahlonega Greer."

Dahlonega. Valdosta endured a pain in her heart every time someone spoke her sister's name. After thirteen years, her sister had been missing from her life longer than she had been a part of it. This was the first solid lead as to her whereabouts since her disappearance. Val had such conflicting emotions. She was elated that it was a lead, but she was devastated that that lead involved blood. Was her sister injured? Was she dead?

As if he were reading her mind, Font said, "The amount of blood was so miniscule that no charges or investigation was ordered. It would have been completely ignored if Elloree wasn't so good at what she does. Since I am not comfortable with her joining the fight anymore, she has agreed to merely do computer research while she is pregnant."

"Be sure to thank her for me," Val said.

"I will."

"Does Willow know about CoZark?" Val asked.

Font looked confused. "Willow? Willow King? What does she have to do with any of this?"

"She is in Haran and I don't know why. I don't know who she is hunting. I want to make sure it isn't CoZark. I don't want him dead and that will be the first thing she tries to do. And, unfortunately, I understand why. But I need him alive. It is the only way I may be able to find out what really happened to my sister."

"If Willow knows about him, it certainly isn't from Elloree or me. We agree with you about how dangerous she is."

Still trying to process all of her emotions, Val nodded slightly.

"I'm about five minutes away from Paedor III. Let's meet at the Downlan and work on our plan of action."

"All right. I'll see you soon. And Val?"

"Yes?"

"Don't worry. We're going to get him this time. And we're going to do it right."

## Chapter 24

"I think I want to marry Willow," Madrick said. Elsinor tried not to react and continued kneading the bread. Of course, she didn't need to make bread by hand. They had two perfectly capable droids that could do it, but she never liked bread made from robots. Call her old-fashioned, but she thought bread kneaded by hand tasted infinitely better.

"You think you want to marry her?" she responded. "That doesn't sound too convincing."

"No, I know I want to marry her; I'm just not sure if it can be. I am not sure she will want me with my humanity and all. There was an incident between us at the lake a couple of weeks ago where she seemed repulsed by my touch."

Elsinor took her hands out of the bowl and wiped them on her apron before clasping the hands of her brother. "Listen to me, Madrick Dashing. I do not care what society says about you. You are a beautiful, talented, brilliant individual. You deserve to love and be loved in return." She wanted to add that he deserved the best and she wasn't sure if Willow was it, but she didn't want to offend her brother. Especially since she had no proof that there was anything wrong with Willow. Nothing more than a woman's intuition. Instead, she kept silent. After releasing Madrick's hands, she went back to making her bread.

"What are you not saying, Elsie?" Madrick asked. She should have known better than to try to conceal her thoughts from her brother.

"Whatever do you mean?"

"I don't know, but something doesn't seem right with you. Do you not approve of Willow?"

"I neither approve nor disapprove," Elsinor said. "I merely feel that you should get to know her better. We barely know anything about her. Who is her family? Why was her estate vacant for nearly three years? How does she know how to drive a car? It's not that I do not like her. It's just that I feel as if I know so little about her."

If Madrick were honest with himself, he would have realized that the concerns expressed by his sister were ones that he shared, especially after that odd encounter with her at the lake. And he still didn't know why she owned an equalizer. Sure, he had fixed it for her, but he never pressed her about its origin or her use for it. He didn't want to be honest with himself, however. He wanted his and

Willow's relationship to be a perfect storybook romance and so he ignored those fears. In fact, it may very well have been those fears that spurred his sudden desire to marry her. "Well, I know her enough for the both of us. I know her better than any other creature on the planet save for you. And I know we belong together," he said stubbornly.

"Okay," Elsinor said simply. She didn't want to argue about this. It was perfectly plausible that he was right. Elsinor could in no way claim to be some sort of expert on love. She had believed that Edgar loved her and she had obviously been erroneous in that estimation.

"I can't believe you feel this way. You don't know her well enough? You know her just as well as you know Val, but if we had been having this exact same conversation about her, you would support a union with her instantly."

Elsinor searched her feelings. He was right. If Madrick had wanted to marry Val, she wouldn't have had any reservations at all. She wondered why that was.

With a shrug Elsinor said, "You are most certainly correct. I would not have this same reaction if we were talking about Val instead of Willow. And I cannot explain the reason for this discrepancy in my feelings so do not ask me to. There is no foundation or basis for my feelings. I just feel that somehow Val is a better match for you. She is open, calm, and sincere. She seems to be your counterbalance but she also seems to have your same wicked sense of humor."

Elsinor transferred her dough to the next bowl and covered it with a towel in order to allow it to rise. "On the other hand, there is something mysterious and almost sinister about Willow. Something hiding behind her smiling eyes. And I can't help but wonder as to why someone would enter into a mutual flirtation just one day after meeting." Elsinor paused. This was not the way she wanted to relay her concerns about Willow, especially after he had just professed his love for her and his desire to be forever united to her. She needed to backtrack and quickly. "Look, Maddie, dear. If you love her, I am sure I will too. I merely need to get to know her better is all."

Madrick smiled but it wasn't his usual broad, gleaming smile that lit up a room. It was an insecure smile filled with doubt. And now Elsinor felt immensely guilty.

"I'm sorry, Maddie. I don't know what is wrong with me. I am sure it is my own misfortune in love that makes me doubt your own felicity with the emotion. Willow is perfectly amiable. And if you love her, please act on your feelings."

This was enough to restore the true brilliance of his smile.

Madrick had mixed emotions as he rode his duster to Willow's estate. Yes, he knew he loved her, but he also valued his sister's opinion more than anyone else's on the planet. Elsinor was the most sensible person Gaion had ever created. Was he missing something in his estimation of Willow?

But then again, while Elsinor was sensible, she was also extremely reserved. She didn't let her emotions out as often as he did. They were siblings but they were completely different. Maybe Elsinor just hadn't experienced a love as strong as what he felt for Willow.

Shrugging off his doubt, he dismounted his duster, determined to follow through with his plan to propose marriage to Willow King.

As he approached her door, he was surprised to see her exiting in a rush.

"Oh, Madrick. What are you doing here?"

"I came to see you," he said, noticing that she didn't seem particularly happy to see him. He also noticed that she was dressed rather oddly. Her clothing was more human than anything even he owned, and he was the one between them that actually had human blood. She was wearing a dress of sorts, but not the tasteful, customary dressing gown common in the islands. In the short, tight outfit she wore, she kind of looked more like she belonged in a paedor. He hated thinking that about his future wife. "Are you going somewhere?"

"Um ... " she said, obviously uncomfortable with the question. "In short, yes. Yes, I am going somewhere. I would rather not expound further." Willow stood on her tiptoes and kissed Madrick on the cheek. "I will return in a few days. Goodbye." She bounded down the stairs and hopped into her car without another word.

And then she was gone. He had half a mind to follow her. Well, actually, he had a full mind to follow her. So that is what he did.

# Chapter 25

Madrick followed Willow to the city limits of Cosmo. He knew he would not be able to travel further. Not dressed the way he was. Cosmo had strict laws on attire. Oddly enough, they only really applied them to humans. Diplomats from other planets and several species common on AiJalon were completely exempt from the dressing requirements either for political or religious reasons. But humans were never afforded such accommodations. If Madrick was not dressed in the proper monochromatic clothing unit, he would immediately be arrested. And what was worse, he didn't even own the proper garment. Having never been to Cosmo in his life, he had neither reason nor opportunity to purchase one. Distraught and disappointed, Madrick turned his duster around and returned home.

Madrick returned to Barton Domicilio quite depressed and quite un-engaged. Elsinor wanted desperately to inquire over what had transpired between the two of them but she also wanted to respect his privacy. She knew that eventually her brother would open up to her. She just had to wait.

Two days later, Madrick still hadn't discussed what happened between him and Willow when they next dined at Barton Hall. The usual levity of the gathering was all but missing. Somehow, the entire party reflected Madrick's woeful mood. It was fascinating to note how much everyone depended on Madrick's engaging personality to somehow set the tone for the evening. Without it, there was only the vexatious rhyming of Comte Middleton undercut by the scathing sarcasm of his wife.

Also, given that both Willow and Val had withdrawn from the island, there were very few people to talk to and very little to talk about. Yes, Lace and Anna Satterly were still there, but they were honestly the last two people on the planet with whom Elsinor wanted to converse. It was this despondent situation that led Mrs. Jensent to make the following recommendation.

"I daresay I cannot stand this melancholy one moment more," she said. "Chai, I believe we need to make our plans known sooner rather than later."

"Oh Mother, do let me tell it. For it is the grandest idea ever," Chai'loi said.

"Well, if it is such a great idea—" the comtesa began.

But Elsinor wisely interrupted her by saying, "Yes, if it is such a great idea, please share with the party." Elsinor was not sure exactly what the comtesa was about to say but she was fairly certain it would not be complimentary. She felt it best to not let the evening slip from somber to spiteful.

"Oh, oh, oh!" Chai'loi said. "It is the best idea ever. The best ever."

"It really is," Mrs. Jensent added. "My only regret in thinking up this idea with my dear Chai is that we didn't think of it sooner."

"That is so true, Mother," Chai'loi said. "Truly the only thing that could make this better would be if we had thought of it yesterday. Or the day before. Or the day—"

"For Gaion's sake just spill it!" Mr. Palmer said suddenly.

An awkward, palpable silence claimed the room as no one knew exactly how to react to Mr. Palmer's outburst.

"Well, do not leave us in suspense," said Comte Middleton suddenly. "Do let us know what thoughts commence."

The comtesa reached for a shot of rum when Mr. Palmer swiped it out of her grasp. She grabbed another and they toasted before simultaneously downing their drinks. Elsinor wondered if Mr. Palmer had joined in on the comtesa's drinking game. Noting how they both seemed equally annoyed at their marriage mates, she also wondered how they ended up in such attachments. Though it was true that most AiJalonian marriages were arranged, she couldn't begin to speculate as to who on AiJalon would pair either the comte and comtesa or Mr. and Mrs. Palmer. But as mismatched as those two couples were, they were much more than Elsinor could ever hope for. She had no social status or financial position to make an attachment to her beneficial for any man. Any marriage that Elsinor could hope for would have to be based in pure love. But even that was no assurance for she was sure her love for Edgar was pure, yet that was obviously for naught.

"It is our design," said Mrs. Jensent finally, "that the young Dashwoods and Satterlys join us in Cosmo for a spell."

"Cosmo?" Madrick said, standing. It was the first all evening he had spoken without being first directly spoken to. Elsinor wasn't sure of the source of his apparent elation, but she could guess it had something to do with Willow.

"That does sound like a lovely idea," Lace said, barely able to contain her own excitement.

Elsinor, for her part, could not think of a more dreadful situation. Trapped in the confining capital with Lace Satterly and the prospect of encountering Edgar was perhaps the worst set of circumstances that she could ever imagine. She had to figure out a way to make sure this was not to be born. "While we are greatly honored by the invitation," began Elsinor, "my brother and I do not have the appropriate attire for Cosmo."

Elsinor could tell that Madrick wanted to protest her protest, but he couldn't as he knew it was true. Even Lace and Anna looked downcast as they, too, obviously did not have the proper attire to reflect their partial human heritage.

"But that is what makes this plan oh so grand," said Mrs. Palmer. "For I did some redecorating of our guest house last month and have several pieces of fabric left over to reflect the correct color clothing units for my human friends. I could have the droids make all of your outfits by tomorrow."

"There you have it, dear sister," Madrick said. "There can be no further objection."

"What about our dear mother?" Elsinor said. "We could not leave her alone with Maggie. She needs our help."

"What am I? Some sort of invalid?" Marzi Dashing asked. "I am perfectly capable of taking care of myself and your sister while you are gone. I insist you go and have a good time in the capital."

179

All in the room stared at Elsinor in silence as if waiting for her approval of the plan. Why did the burden fall on her? She didn't want to disappoint her brother as he obviously wanted to see his Willow, but she also did not fancy the idea of perhaps running into Edgar. In fact, she dreaded the idea. Unfortunately, there was no way to protest further without raising suspicion. So, she merely nodded her acquiescence, thus sending the Satterly girls and Mrs. Palmer into bloodcurdling squeals and giggles.

"If you could celebrate a little louder, Chai'loi, I don't believe they heard you on Tentor," Mr. Palmer said.

# Chapter 26

"Honestly, Elsie, what is wrong with you?" Madrick took a moment to glance up the stairs probably to make sure his mother and younger sister were out of hearing range. "If you had invented one more unnecessary obstacle to our jaunt to Cosmo I might have had to shake some sense into you."

Elsinor pretended to inspect a droid. She couldn't look at her brother. Not now. One look in her eyes and he would see her pain. She didn't want to have to explain how she was now permanently separated from the only man she had ever loved. "Just trying to be practical," she said, forcing her voice to have a lilt of ease.

"Dear sister. Always the picture of practicality. Always the perfect sense for sensibility. Where is your feeling? Surely you must want to see Edgar as much as I want to see Willow."

Another flash of pain seared her heart. Not only was she separated from Edgar, now she was emotionally separating herself from her beloved brother. Her confidant and best friend. In that moment, she felt profoundly alone.

Blinking away a possible onslaught of tears, she said, "My desires and feelings are irrelevant when in the service of the greater good. We have a mother and a younger sister. Who are to care for them in our absence?"

"Gaion, Elsie. As Mother noted, they are not invalids. They can care for themselves for a few days."

Elsinor turned the droid she had been inspecting off and then turned it on again for no particular reason besides she needed something to do with her hands while she tried not to respond to her brother.

"Is something wrong with the droid?" Madrick asked finally when Elsinor didn't continue the conversation. He knelt next to her and inspected it as well.

Standing, Elsinor said, "In any case, it seems I am outvoted. I suppose we are headed to Cosmo," before heading upstairs.

\*\*\*

The party left for Cosmo even earlier than Elsinor expected. She had hoped it would take a few days to make the appropriate attire, but Mrs.

Jensent's droid apparently worked through the night. Thus, by the time the first sun rose, both Madrick and Elsinor had received TelExes indicating they should be ready to leave within the hour.

Madrick was up and about so quickly Elsinor wasn't sure he had been to sleep at all the evening prior.

Riding in Mrs. Jensent's guster with Lace and Anna was almost unbearable. They would not stop talking even for a moment. Elsinor had hoped that her brother would realize her discomfort and alleviate the consistent barrage of conversation she was currently enduring, but Madrick was lost in his own world of thoughts. After the third time he checked his TelEx, Elsinor wondered if he had been in contact with Willow and was waiting for a communication from her.

"What do you think we will do first when we get there?" Anna asked.

"Oh, I don't know," Lace answered. "There is so much to do in Cosmo. I have made a list. Would you like to see, Elsinor?"

"Not really."

"Oh, I can bet what is on the top of that list," Anna said as if neither of them had heard Elsinor's response. Anna smiled knowingly at her sister.

"Anna, stop that. I have no idea what you are inferring."

"Of course you do. It pertains to a certain young man who has earned your favor."

Not being able to avoid conversation that involved young men, Mrs. Jensent just had to join in. "A young man, you say? What young man has caught my young cousin's fancy? What sort of man is he?"

"Oh, he is the best sort of man," Anna began.

"Anna, don't be ridiculous. You know there is no such man," Lace said quickly as she gave her sister a chastising look.

"I do?" Anna asked.

"Yes, you do."

"Oh, right. I do. There is no such man."

"Ah well," Mrs. Jensent said. "If I have anything to do with it, there will be such a man for all of you very shortly." Before turning her attention away she added, "And I haven't forgotten about you, Mr. Madrick Dashing. I am sure your Willow is in Cosmo just waiting to see you. She will be so excited at your surprise presence."

From the way Madrick looked longingly at his TelEx, Elsinor was not too sure of that prediction.

# Chapter 27

"Well look at this," Mrs. Jensent said, staring at her TelEx the next morning at breakfast. "Not even a full day in Cosmo and we have already received our first invitation." Lace and Anna's eyes lit up at the proposal. Elsinor could not care less for invitations anywhere. For either Edgar would be there or Edgar wouldn't be there. She couldn't quite determine which would be the worse fate. Though her head knew she was forever separated from him, her heart yearned to see him again and ached for a better outcome. Maybe just the sight of her would cause him to forsake his family and his obligations to Lace and declare his undying love for her. She knew it wasn't possible. She knew she would perhaps even respect him less if he carelessly relinquished the duty of his promises. But she could dream.

Madrick, too, did not care for invitations anywhere. From what he could tell, Willow King did not run in the same circles as the people who would invite Mrs. Jensent to a gathering. He had no confidence that he would see her at any kind of summit or festivity Cosmo had to offer. In fact, he wondered what had really brought her to Cosmo in the first place. He couldn't shake the suspicion that Willow was hiding something from him.

"What is the invitation?" Anna asked. "Is it a summit? Will there be dancing?"

"There will be dancing, of a sort, and much more. We have been invited to the CHG. The Championship Hafenstat Gala."

The Satterlys squealed in delight. Even Madrick perked up a bit at this prospect.

"Is this going to be held at the Twilex?" he asked.

Mrs. Jensent looked at her TelEx again. "Yes, yes it is. Why?"

"The Twilex is next door to the Parque Hotel," he added.

"And what does that mean?" Elsinor asked.

"Nothing. Nothing at all." Madrick gathered his TelEx and headed upstairs without saying another word.

"What is that about?" asked Mrs. Jensent. Elsinor shrugged. "Anyway," she continued, "the gala is of course before the game and in Cosmo. The invitation includes tickets to the match itself on the island of Jander! Have any of you seen a professional hafenstat game?"

Elsinor did not hear the response from the Satterlys as she was too focused on her brother. She excused herself and followed him upstairs.

"Dearest," she said as she knocked on his door, "may I come in?" When there was no answer, she took it upon herself to enter. She found her brother slumped over what looked like a broken TelEx with wires exposed. He had a wild look in his eye as he frantically screwed in wires and pressed buttons.

"Maddie?"

"Yesterday as we drove through the town," he began, not taking his eyes off of his work, "I got a signal as we passed the Parque Hotel. I think she's there."

"A signal? What kind of signal? Is this about Willow?" That was a stupid question. Of course, it was about Willow. Everything regarding Madrick had been about Willow for the past several weeks. "Maddie, what are you talking about?"

"Before we left Haran, I reconfigured my TelEx to connect with the coordinates of her TelEx so I could find her. It didn't work. Or I thought it didn't work. Not until we passed the Parque Hotel. There must be a range issue. I think I can fix it. And if I can get it done before the hafenstat game tonight, I will be able to know exactly where she is by the time we get there."

Elsinor sighed. Her brother was behaving completely mad. She had to figure out a way to politely make him see this. "Madrick dear, have you sent her a message on the TelEx?"

"Yes, of course I have."

"And has she responded?" Madrick didn't answer. "And how many messages have you sent her?"

"I know I seem senseless," he said finally.

"I didn't say that."

"But you thought it. Sometimes love makes you do crazy things. You would know that if you had ever been in—" He stopped and looked at her.

"Are you assuming I have never been in love or perhaps that I am incapable of love?"

"That is not what I was trying to say."

Elsinor stood to leave.

"I am merely saying that what Willow and I have is so much stronger than anything—"

"Stop, Madrick. You have said enough."

\*\*\*

The Twilex was the most famous ballroom on the planet. Of course, it was not originally built for such festivities. It was originally the meeting place of the AiJalonian council which included a representative from one of each of the founding twelve families of AiJalon. As the influence of other more festive cultures infiltrated the planet and the governance of the planet shifted to the different ministries, the Twilex was converted into a gorgeous ballroom. Upon entering, Elsinor felt the checkered floors, domed ceilings and arched entryways resembled something out of an ancient Shakespeare play. But she could have been confusing the architecture for something more out of Earth's Renaissance period. She always confused those ancient time periods. The elaborate gowns from the islands would have been more appropriate in the Twilex. Instead, having people walk around in monochromatic clothing units seemed odd and stark. It exacerbated the difficult circumstance that AiJalon as a whole found itself in trying to combine propriety and tradition with a morphing culture and civilization.

"I've been doing research on the Cosmo elite all day and anyone who is anyone is going to be here," Lace said.

"Look, look, look! That includes your future family," Anna said, pointing to Femili Fyatt Dashing.

Lace's eyes grew. "Anna, you really have to watch what you say in public." Both Anna and Lace began to look around nervously.

"Be at ease," Elsinor said. "It is so crowded here, I don't believe anyone heard you besides myself."

After breathing a sigh of relief, Lace locked arms with Elsinor and said, "I am so fortunate to have a friend like you to confide in during my time of distress."

"Why are you distressed? Shouldn't you be rejoicing at the prospect of seeing your beloved?"

"Well, yes, of course I am. But I am also a bit nervous. I am sure you can understand why. All of my future happiness relies on Edgar's family accepting me and my genetics. What should happen if they do not?"

"Edgar is an honorable man. He will keep his vow to you whether his family approves or not."

"Oh, Elsinor. From your lips to Gaion's ears."

"Look who I found, girls," Mrs. Jensent said. For a moment, Elsinor's heart caught in her chest as she thought Mrs. Jensent could be referring to Edgar. But once she noticed she was merely referring to her daughter Chai'loi, Elsinor realized how ridiculous she was being. Mrs. Jensent didn't even know what Edgar looked like.

"It is ever so good to see you," Chai'loi said. "What a fortunate invitation for us all. I have a feeling the invitation has more to do with the young Dashings than it does with us, Mother."

"What do you mean?" Elsinor asked.

"Well, Femili Fyatt Dashing was on the planning committee and from what I hear, she was determined to make sure you and your brother were invited. Where is your brother by the way?" Chai'loi asked.

Realizing she hadn't seen Madrick since they stepped off the tobulin outside of the Twilex, Elsinor started looking around. Her search abruptly ended when she heard Mrs. Jensent say, "Oh look. There is Femili Fyatt Dashing now! Femili, Femili, over here."

Elsinor could tell from the look on Femili's face that the very last thing she wanted to do was talk to Mrs. Jensent. But given that she was practically yelling across the gallery, there was nothing else socially acceptable for her to do but acknowledge the beckoning.

"Well, hello," Femili said. "You must be Mrs. Jensent."

"And I know you, Femili Fyatt Dashing. I must compliment you on the festivities tonight. Such an excellent gathering."

"Oh, I thank you. I cannot take all the credit. My mother helped in the arrangements."

"What a gracious daughter," Mrs. Jensent said. "Let me introduce you to my own daughter, Chai'loi. And my cousins, the misses Satterly. And I am sure you know your sister-in-law."

"Why yes, of course, I know my husband's HALF-sister." Femili was sure to emphasize the half part. "Where is your brother?"

"I am actually not sure at the moment," Elsinor responded.

"Well, speaking of brothers, here is mine."

Lace squeezed Elsinor's arm in anticipation of seeing Edgar. Elsinor dared not turn around. She finally determined the worse of the two fates. Seeing him for the first time in a month in front of the woman he was betrothed to marry would break what was left of her heart.

An hour passed in a matter of seconds. Finally, Femili's brother approached and she said, "May I introduce my youngest brother, Mr. Roymond Fyatt?"

Elsinor felt as if she had dodged a specially aimed bullet trained on her heart. She breathed relief.

"Ah, the first young man of the evening," Mrs. Jensent said. "I present before you three fine young single ladies. I do say you must choose one to dance with. What say you start with Miss Dashing?"

"Actually, I think I must go find my brother," Elsinor said, happy to have an excuse. Even if her brother did not need to be located she was in no way in the mood to dance.

"In that case, may I have the honor of dancing with you?" Roymond said to Lace.

"Why, yes. Yes, of course." Roymond took Lace's hand and led her to the nearest table where they sat down to begin their "dance."

Within the city limits of Cosmo, real dancing was thought to be inappropriate. Much too much contact between the sexes. Thus, a Cosmo summit consisted of virtual dancing. Two people sat across from each other at a small table and put on their CSA or Cosmo Summit Accouterment, which included sensory gloves and goggles which simulated dancing. This process was supposed to be more sophisticated and pure but Elsinor had heard many stories about adjustments being made to the CSA and couples being able to simulate much more than dancing right there in public. In any case, it was not the kind of thing that interested Elsinor.

Elsinor spent the rest of the evening searching for her brother. For a while, she thought that maybe he was already dancing with someone in the Twilex, but after looking at every table she concluded that he could not be in the building. Remembering that Madrick had mentioned something about the Parque Hotel, Elsinor had just decided to wander over there briefly when she was suddenly flanked on both sides by Lace and her sister.

"Elsinor, Elsinor, we have the best news there is! I can barely contain myself," Lace said.

"Oh? Is Edgar here?"

"No, it is even better than Edgar being here."

Elsinor briefly wondered what could be better than seeing his face again. She couldn't come up with anything.

"It is his mother," Lace said

"Oh?"

"And not only is she here, but she has invited the three of us to watch the hafenstat game from her hoverbox!"

"I have never been in a hoverbox," Anna said. "I am going to feel so fancy."

"And rich," Lace added. "Do you have any idea how much those cost?"

"Yes, they are quite expensive," was all Elsinor could think to say. She was too busy wondering why on AiJalon Mrs. Fyatt would invite her of all people to her hoverbox. But the calculated reason for this invitation became clear rather quickly.

# Chapter 28

"Can you believe we have been invited to the hafenstat meet by Edgar's mother and sister?" Lace said excitedly as they waited for the tobulin outside of the Twilex. "I am so nervous. I mean they are soon to be my family. And you know what they say about first impressions."

"Yes, yes I do." Elsinor tried her best to ignore the ramblings of Lace Satterly and just nodded in agreement whenever she felt it was appropriate.

She desperately wished her brother was there to help her endure this, but he was still nowhere to be found. Even if he was around, he wouldn't have been allowed in a hoverbox with all women. No, Elsinor was condemned to suffer this evening on her own. She wondered what she had done in her past to deserve this punishment from Gaion himself.

Moments after boarding the hoverbox and rising into the air, Anna Satterly looked quite ill.

"Are you all right, Anna?" Elsinor asked.

"Yes, yes, I am fine," she said unconvincingly as she grabbed the back of a seat firmly. "I just had no idea it would be so high."

"Yes, the box has to fly quite high so as not to potentially interfere with the game. But we are not as high as we were in the guster that brought us to Cosmo."

"A guster does not have a glass floor."

"That is true."

"I think I'm going to be sick."

And thus, the evening began with Anna Satterly vomiting into the trash compactor. The first casualty of the hoverbox, a ridiculous innovation from the planet Lumerca.

It was the single most outlandish and expensive manner to watch a sporting event. So far, that is. Elsinor was convinced that one day the wealthy Lumercans would concoct another gadget to convince the rest of the galaxy they needed to buy.

A hoverbox was a luxury room that fit about fifteen people. Instead of being stationary and permanently part of a sporting venue, it floated above the players and allowed for the best vantage point at every moment in the game. Everyone sat in their comfortable chairs and watched the action through a glass floor while being served food and beverages by droids.

It was a completely inefficient, dangerous and downright stupid way to watch a game. The box moved constantly, often causing people to spill their food or others to become sick to their stomach. It was merely a status symbol and often used as a way to demean people.

For example, Mrs. Fyatt in particular seemed to use the hoverbox as a sort of weapon, ordering it to shift or move, not based on where the ball happened to be during a certain play, but rather on who she could embarrass by making them drop their food. Though not a particularly tall woman, she had a way of looking down on everyone as she wore her extremely dark, monochromatic clothing unit representing her remarkably pure AiJalonian bloodline. Every time she shifted the direction of the box, a small smirk formed on her lips as she stole a glance at Elsinor. Ironically, the shifting levels and directions did not affect her as expected. The one most affected was Anna Satterly who was bent over in a corner trying to keep from vomiting ... again.

"Oh, Elsinor, did you drop your purple fial biscuit?" Femili Fyatt Dashing asked. "Shall I fetch a droid to make you another plate of food? You know, not everyone has the adequate breeding to keep their balance in a machine like this."

"That may be because hoverboxes were not actually designed to watch hafenstat games and have been proven to be quite impractical. They were created on Lumerca to watch underwater sports."

"That is the complaint of some people regarding hoverboxes," began Mrs. Fyatt, "but I think those that complain are the ones who do not have the elegance to properly use them."

Elsinor could see clearly through the poorly veiled insult. All evening, Edgar and Femili's mother had taken every opportunity to insult her. It was obvious the only reason they invited her to this event was to ensure that Elsinor knew that she was not and would never be accepted as a member of the Fyatt family.

"You know, last week, I had Miss Amelia Morton here with me in this very hoverbox," Mrs. Fyatt said.

"Oh? The lovely Miss Amelia Morton? I bet she didn't complain of the impracticality of hoverboxes," Femili said.

"Of course not," said Mrs. Fyatt. "Miss Amelia Morton is always the picture of elegance and class."

"I would love to one day be able to call her sister," Femili added, obviously to enrage Elsinor. "Wouldn't she make a remarkable addition to the family, Mother?"

Because Elsinor had already resolved in her heart that she could never be with Edgar and thus never be a Fyatt, the comment did not succeed in its intended effort. It could not possibly make Elsinor feel any worse than she already did. Lace, on the other hand, was quite affected by it. Elsinor noticed a sadness befall her normally cheery expression.

Though slightly sad, Lace was in no way willing to accept defeat. "Miss Morton sounds like a lovely woman. I am sure she would be an excellent addition to your family," Lace said in a sickeningly sweet voice.

"What a nice thing to say," said Mrs. Fyatt. "What was your name again dear?"

"Lace. Lace Satterly."

"I see you are having no problem with the hoverbox," she continued. "You must have the excellent breeding that some people so desperately lack."

Elsinor could only roll her eyes at the overt insult that was especially ludicrous considering Lace's own sister was currently vomiting in the trash compactor. Some breeding.

"Yes, my friend, Lace, is only one quarter human, one quarter Engorian, and half AiJalonian," Femili said.

Friend? When did they get so close? They had only met that evening. Elsinor reasoned that Femili would consider a sea monster from Tentor a friend over Elsinor herself.

Lace, for her part, just beamed at that terminology in reference to herself. Surely, she assumed she was getting closer and closer to being accepted into the Fyatt family.

"A very fine mix indeed," Mrs. Fyatt said. "Not too much humanity to spoil your general elegance."

"Oh, thank you, ma'am," Lace said sweetly. "I hope that one day some of your regal demeanor will somehow transfer to me just by being in your presence."

This conversation was becoming downright insane. As if elegance and balance had anything to do with species and as if you could develop either through some sort of spatial osmosis. For her own sanity, Elsinor removed herself from the balance of this conversation and settled on taking care of Anna.

# Chapter 29

He shouldn't have followed her to Cosmo. She was his love and he should have trusted her to love him back and be loyal. But her behavior was so odd that he couldn't resist the urge. Willow couldn't be cheating on him, could she? Not when he was about to pour his heart out to her and ask her to be his wife.

But when he saw his Willow walking hand in hand with a man through the hotel lobby he knew the truth. She didn't love him. She was with another man. Maybe she loved him more.

He shouldn't have been surprised. Madrick Dashing the human. What was he expecting? There was no logical reason why a beautiful AiJalonian woman would ever want a half-human mistura like himself.

He felt equal parts pain, sadness and anger. But in that moment, the anger won out. Madrick stormed to the center of the hotel lobby to confront her.

"This is why you left Haran last week?" a voice asked. The pain in her chest told her immediately that it was Madrick. What on AiJalon was he doing in Cosmo? Had he followed her?

Willow turned around slowly. And in an overwhelmingly composed voice that apparently made Madrick even more furious said, "Madrick, I need you to calm down."

"Calm down? You want me to calm down? Willow, I love you. I love you more than any woman I have ever met. And now I see you with another man. I cannot and will not calm down."

"Madrick, this is not what it looks like. I can explain things but not here and not now."

"I don't want any explanation from you. I was going to ask you to marry me that day. But instead you run off to be with another man."

"Wait, you want to marry me?"

"Of course I do."

For a moment, Willow was frozen in thought. "You really love me?" she asked. She knew what she felt for Madrick was unlike anything she had ever felt in her life. She knew she loved him but wasn't sure anyone would ever really love her in return. But he did. He loved her. Someone actually found her worthy of love. But it would be fleeting. She had a feeling that after this night, no matter the outcome, any chance of happiness she had with Madrick would be destroyed.

"Of course, I do." Madrick looked at the man next to Willow. "Well, I did. Now I am not so sure."

"Madrick, I promise there is an explanation. You—"

"What kind of explanation can there be? You are in a hotel with a man."

"Is there a problem here?" a servant droid asked. Willow looked around the lobby and noticed that they were causing a scene. All eyes were on them. This was not the kind of attention she needed. She could not be seen with a man who was about to be found dead in his hotel room.

"Sit here. Don't move," she instructed CoZark. He obeyed with a smile. "Come with me, Maddie," Willow said, grabbing his hand. Maybe she could get him to wait for her in the bar while she got CoZark to his room. She would have to rethink his execution. It would be too risky to do it after this commotion in such a public place.

"No!" He dropped her hand and took a step toward CoZark. "What kind of hold does she have on you that you do exactly what she says?" Madrick asked him.

"Is the human causing a problem?" the droid asked.

"No, he's not."

"I have notified the authorities," the droid said.

Willow took deep breaths to calm her nerves. How did the situation get this out of control? All she wanted to do was complete her mission and rid the planet of one more miscreant that no one needed. Now the galactic police were likely on the way and she would likely be caught and imprisoned. She had to get out of there. Her mission as Gaion's angel was in jeopardy.

She didn't have time to take CoZark back to his room and torture him like she usually did her victims. But he still needed to die. She also didn't want to lose this opportunity. She had no idea when the next time she would be able to find him. He had to die tonight. So as she saw the galactic police enter the lobby, she decided to improvise.

"For someone so brilliant you really can be impossibly daft," Willow said before pulling him close and kissing him on the lips. "I'm sorry, Madrick. I have to do this," she added when she let him up for air.

"What?" he asked.

"You monster!" she screamed before slapping him in the face. "Here he is, IGP," she said to the officers. Immediately, the two galactic police officers, who looked like they were both part Harvothite and thus very large, took Madrick in to custody.

"What is going on? I didn't do anything."

As Madrick was being arrested, Willow slipped away. Discreetly, she pulled an equalizer from out of her jacket. All eyes were on Madrick so she was in no danger of being seen as she fired a single bullet into the back of CoZark's head.

# Chapter 30

When the party disembarked from the hoverbox on Jandor, they found Val waiting for them.

"Val?" Elsinor asked. "What are you doing here? We haven't seen you since you left Haran in a rush."

"You need to come with me immediately, Elsinor," Val said as she turned and started walking away briskly.

"What? Why?" Elsinor asked as she started following Val. "What's going on?" Suddenly, Elsinor got a really bad feeling. "Is this about Madrick?"

Val gave an almost imperceptible nod, then said, "Your brother has been arrested," as she stepped into her private guster.

"Arrested? For what?"

"All I could gather from my contacts is that he had an argument with Willow at the Parque Hotel and the intergalactic police were called."

"Argument? I don't understand. What were they fighting about? Why did he need to get arrested for it? Surely the police understand that it was just a lovers' quarrel."

Val sighed. "There's more." Val opened up her mouth to speak but no words formed. "I don't actually know where to begin. But it is a twenty-minute ride back to Cosmo. Perhaps I can explain in that amount of time."

Elsinor waited patiently as Val apparently searched for the right words to begin her tale.

"Willow King and I have known each other ... No, let me start further back. When I was ten years old, my sister disappeared. I later learned that she was kidnapped and sold to slavers in a paedor."

Elsinor gasped. "Oh, Val. I am so sorry."

"What hurt more than knowing my sister was out in the galaxy somewhere suffering was the fact that no one was looking for her. No one even talked about the slave trade on this planet. It was as if people thought if they just ignored it, it would go away. I couldn't live with that. So I started searching for my sister. At that young age, there wasn't much I could do, but as I got older, and stronger, and wiser, I learned how to help these forgotten girls of the slave trade. One of those forgotten girls was Willow."

"Willow? Willow King? Willow was a paedor slave?"

"Not because of any wrongdoing on her part. She was kidnapped by a man named Ge'or Wixsum who promised her love and marriage. But Willow is strong and smart. I was on my way to try to rescue her when she managed to forge her own escape. I later found her and helped her rebuild her life after such a harrowing ordeal. I thought teaching her self-defense would help her regain her confidence and self-esteem."

"It didn't?"

"No, it did. Too well. She began having wild delusions."

"Like what?"

Val sighed. "Willow truly believes that she is Gaion's executioner, the chosen one to fulfill prophecy. And as such, she feels complete authority to exact his judgment on any and all who participate in the slave trade."

"What do you mean?" Elsinor asked as a sickening feeling developed in her stomach.

"I mean she's a murderer. And her first victim was Ge'or Wixsum. Since then she has murdered eleven men connected to the slave trade. And a few that were wholly unconnected and one in particular who—" Val suddenly became emotional.

Elsinor was curious as to who the man was that was wholly unconnected. She had the feeling it was someone close to Val, but she didn't want to pry. Thankfully, she didn't have to.

"Milo was my fiancée. A little over a year ago, we were working together on a mission to free a shipment of girls on Capernica. Willow had other plans. Her main focus isn't the girls, it is revenge. Willow and her band of mercenaries ambushed us and the shipment in an effort to murder the ringleader of the organization. She might not have meant to have us killed, but when you make backdoor dealings with criminals, you put everyone's life at risk."

"So Milo was killed?"

Val nodded. "A specter blast. He never knew what hit him."

"And what about your sister? Did you ever find out anything about her?"

"For thirteen years, I have scoured the galaxy in search of her and helped save as many girls as I could along the way. Then four days ago, a blood sample matching that of my sister was found aboard the vessel of Leaven CoZark in Paedor III."

"Four days ago? Is that why you left the party?"

"It is. I needed to follow this new piece of information. It is the only link I have had to my sister in thirteen years."

There were so many questions that Elsinor wanted to ask, but she could tell this was a painful topic for Val. So instead she asked, "What does all of this have to do with my brother?"

"I am convinced," Val began, "that CoZark is Willow's next target. I found him in Cosmo and then mere hours later, Willow was also there. The problem is, we have different philosophies about how he should be dealt with. For Willow, everything is black and white. He has bought and sold women and therefore he must die."

"And you don't agree?"

"If I am honest with myself ...Yes. I do agree. I want him dead. But I also want to know what happened to my sister. If he is dead, how will I ever find out what happened to her? In any case, I speculate that Willow was in Cosmo trying to lure CoZark into some sort of trap. Madrick found them and created some sort of scene and got himself arrested. Hopefully, that is all that has occurred and we can clear up the situation quickly. If not, I am not sure what we will have to do."

By the time Val and Elsinor arrived at the hotel where the entire commotion started, Madrick and the intergalactic police had already left.

"Wait here. I am going to try to find out what has happened," Val said.

Even though Elsinor was wearing the appropriate clothing attire, she still felt as though everyone was staring at her in the expensive hotel. Was it because she was human? Was it because she looked a bit like Madrick? She couldn't decide. In any case, she felt extremely out of place and wanted to leave immediately.

Crime was so rare on AiJalon and almost completely relegated to the paedors. Whenever crime did occur outside of the paedors, it always seemed to comfort the inhabitants of AiJalon if that crime was a result of human activity. It was as if it justified their treatment and prejudice toward the species.

Elsinor tried to ignore the looks of disdain she received from the hotel guests and waited patiently for Val.

"It is worse than we thought," she said once she had returned.

"How?" Elsinor asked.

"Apparently, CoZark was murdered right here in this lobby just moments ago."

"Oh no, you won't be able to ask him about your sister."

Val shook her head. "Don't worry about my sister right now. What is important is your brother."

"Why?"

"Because the intergalactic police think he did it."

"How can that be? My brother would never hurt anyone. Oh, I understand," Elsinor said as things became clear. "It is because he's human, isn't it?"

"Partly," Val responded.

"What do you mean 'partly'? That he is part human or that I am part right?"

"I mean you are part right. I am sure the authorities completely believe he is capable of murder because he is human. But they also have more cause than that."

"What can they possibly have?"

"Apparently, Willow set him up to take the fall for this."

"I don't ... That can't ... Why would she do that? She loves him."

"Not as much as her freedom. Not as much as her bloodthirsty desire for vengeance. I'm sorry but it is true."

Elsinor tried to reconcile these words with what she had seen of Willow over the past month. She knew there was something unsettling about how fast and fierce Willow's romance with Madrick was, but she never thought there was anything malicious in her intent.

# Chapter 31

"How can they possible think Madrick had anything to do with this?" Elsinor asked as they reentered the guster. "It's not possible. He doesn't even possess an equalizer and never has."

"That doesn't matter," Val said. "What matters is that Madrick is a human who was seen fighting with a woman whom I assume was Willow, who was with CoZark. From that bit of information alone, it is enough to assume that CoZark and Madrick were fighting over Willow and that Madrick killed him because of it."

"But that's no fair."

"Life isn't fair. That is something I have learned the hard way over the past few years. In any case, the evidence is flimsy and it will never hold up in court. But right now, we have a bigger problem."

"What can be bigger than my brother being arrested for murder?"

"The fact that most likely he will never make it to trial alive."

"What are you talking about?"

"As of right now, CoZark's men believe that Madrick killed him. They are undoubtedly on their way to intercept the prisoner transport in order to seek revenge for their master."

"You mean, they are going to hurt Madrick?"

"Not if we get to him first."

Elsinor's stomach nearly lurched into her throat as Val took to speeds that were highly illegal within the city limits. "If you're caught piloting this guster at such a speed, you could be subject to severe fines," Elsinor said in hopes that Val would slow down somewhat.

Val shrugged. "I have more money than I know what to do with. A few fines will do virtually no damage to my bank account."

That was not the response she was hoping for. "Why are you doing this?" she asked.

"Doing what?"

"Going through all this trouble to help my brother, a human. This has nothing to do with you. You could easily be back in Haran resting in your guest room at Barton Manor."

"CoZark has plenty to do with me. He is the key to finding out what happened to my sister."

"But he's dead now. And you're still going after Madrick. Why?" Deep down, Elsinor knew the

214

answer. Val was in love with her brother. She just wanted to hear her say it. It gave her hope in the concept of love which she had all but given up on. Now that Edgar was forever separated from her, at times she had begun to feel love didn't exist at all.

"I ... um ..." Val stuttered. "I do not like to see injustice of any kind. What is about to happen to your brother is a gross injustice."

"Don't get me wrong, I am forever grateful to you. I would not have the first clue what to do in this situation to help him. I just feel like there is another reason why you are determined to be of assistance to him."

There was a long pause as the guster hurtled through the air at a sickening speed. Finally, Val said, "I see Milo in him."

"What?"

"Madrick is the first person to ever remind me of Milo. His smile, his determination, his spirit. How he almost magically understands nearly anything he encounters. He truly is special."

"Have you told him this?"

Val paused. "I almost did once. It was the day he met Willow. But once he met her, I feel like I lost any chance." She shook her head as if trying to shake reason into herself. "Doesn't matter really. There is no way he would ever be interested in me."

"Val, I wouldn't—"

"There!" she said, interrupting her. "There is the prisoner transport ship."

"It looks empty."

"It's not." In one swift movement, Val simultaneously stopped the guster, pulled out some sort of electric device that was a cross between a sword and a baton, and jumped out of the vehicle.

A prisoner transport vehicle was like a guster but more than twice as big. Elsinor had never actually seen one in person, just heard about them.

Elsinor watched as Val entered the transport vehicle, sword drawn. She had no idea Val owned a sword or was capable of handling one. And she had absolutely no idea why she needed one now. A part of her wanted to follow, but she was afraid.

\*\*\*

As she slowly made her way through the vehicle, Val tried to evaluate what had happened while staying alert enough to defend herself in the event of an attack. And she was sure an attack was eminent. In fact, she hoped for one. If there was an attack, it meant Madrick was still alive.

Val speculated that the entire vehicle was hit with a nomaray, which would knock out all of its power and render all of the inhabitants temporarily immobilized. A nomaray was a common weapon on most planets, but not on CoZark's planet, Kemek.

She wondered if these were really CoZark's men after all.

Steps echoed in the hull. They were not her own. They were getting closer and faster. But from the sound of the steps, she could tell it was only one person. And the weight distribution was off. This person was not a Regavite like CoZark. They were second in size to the Harvothites.

Val struck an opposition pose and said, "Don't move, Willow."

"Why are you here, Val?" Willow responded as she raised her own weapon. "This doesn't concern you."

"Put down the equalizer," Val said.

"Why?"

"First, because you're not going to shoot me. Second, because the core is set to change in less than two minutes and it will be useless."

"If I wanted to shoot you, you know I would need much, much less time than that. You know how good my aim is."

"I know a lot of things about you. Too many things. I should end you right now."

"But you won't. That is the difference between you and me. You are not strong enough to do what is needed when it is needed. You would have let CoZark live."

"CoZark was the only link to my sister. I needed him alive. He could have been the key to finding her."

"Gaion, Valdosta! Do you really think she's still alive? It's been thirteen years."

"I had hope. Now I have nothing once again because of you!"

Willow paused. "I'm sorry for Milo. I should have said that a year ago. I didn't mean for that to happen."

"Well, it did. And if you go on crusading around the galaxy like some sort of vengeful demon, more innocent people will die."

"Sometimes sacrifices must be made for the greater good."

"Do you hear yourself? Do you really believe this sanctimonious coddle swak? This is not why I trained you."

"You are one to call someone sanctimonious, Valdosta Greer. You think you are too pure to take someone's life? Do you really think you are fixing anything by letting these men live? They are just going to hurt other girls."

"You don't know that. They can change."

"Val, we will never agree about this. Let's just do what we came here for. Let's save—"

"What are you two doing here?" Madrick himself said, interrupting them. His hands were still bound and he was uneasy on his feet. He swayed and Valdosta grabbed his shirt to keep him vertical.

"Madrick, how are you even conscious?" Valdosta asked.

"The nomaray isn't as effective on the human nervous system as it is on other species." He blinked his eyes rapidly and shook his head. "Just as painful but not as long-lasting."

"I'm so happy you are all right," Willow said, going to embrace him.

Madrick stepped away from her. "Don't touch me," he said.

"Whyever not?" Willow asked.

Before she could answer, Valdosta heard the distinctive sound of a Regavite musket. "Everybody down," she said, pushing them both to the floor as a stream of blue light shot above their heads and tore a hole into the side of the guster. "They're here," she said. "And they're armed."

On hands and knees, they followed Val into a small equipment locker.

"How many?" Willow asked as she pushed a button on her equalizer and pulled another one from an ankle holster.

"Six—no." Valdosta paused. "Seven."

"How can she tell?" Madrick asked.

"She has very good hearing," Willow responded. "Have you ever handled one of these?" she asked, holding an equalizer out for him.

Madrick held up his hands that were still bound by an electric band. "Might be easier if I—"

"Val?"

"Got it." Val lifted her sword and swiped it down right on top of the cuffs, breaking them in two.

Madrick didn't even have time to process the fact that a rich AiJalonian heiress had just sliced his handcuffs in half with a sword that could have sliced his hands off if moved a hair's length in either direction.

Willow slapped the equalizer into his hand and said, "I ask you again, can you use one of these?"

It was kind of a ridiculous question since this was the exact equalizer that he had adjusted for her. Did she think he could fix it and then would not know how to use it? "I can figure it out," he assured her.

"There's no time to figure it out." Val looked at a device on her wrist. "You have forty-seven seconds before the core shifts."

"That's all I need," Willow said before jumping back into the corridor.

"Willow!" Val called out after her.

"What is she doing?" Madrick asked.

"Trying to get herself killed," Val said before leaping after her.

\*\*\*

Madrick could distinguish the sounds easier than he thought he would be able to. The Regavite muskets sounded like the laser-like whizz of when a guster powered up. The equalizer made a popping noise like when the engine in an antique car misfired. And then there was the clank of Val's sword hitting what Madrick suspected was the chest armor of the Regavites.

"Willow, time!" he heard Val call. He knew she meant Willow was running out of time to use her equalizer. Madrick looked down at the one she had handed him. It meant his would be useless soon as well. He had to figure out a way to help them immediately. He stared at the odd buttons on the device, flipped it over a couple of times, and as it usually happened with Madrick Dashing, everything seemed to click.

Madrick stepped into the corridor. Four men were already lying unconscious on the floor. One was obviously dead from a bullet wound to the head. The other three could have still been alive. Madrick decided immediately that if he did fire this equalizer, he would not be aiming to kill.

Willow was in hand-to-hand combat with one Regavite while Val fought off two simultaneously. Willow was obviously unable to get a good shot off and was struggling to subdue her opponent.

Aiming for the Regavite's lower back, Madrick pointed and fired. The Regavite let go of Willow in order to clutch his side, allowing Willow to get free. She stepped back and aimed for his head.

"No!" Madrick yelled.

She pulled the trigger but nothing happened. The equalizer was now useless. Instead, Willow kicked him in the head and knocked him out. Next, she took his musket. Turning around, she aimed at the two men fighting Val.

"No," Madrick yelled again, afraid that Willow would miss and hit Val. She didn't miss.

"Why did you do that?" Val asked, panting from the exertion of her fight.

"Do what? Save you?"

"Kill them? I could have defeated them. They didn't have to die."

"Gaion, Val. Save your life and all I get is a lecture. Next time I'll just let them kill you."

"There won't be a next time," Val said. She lifted her sword. "I'm taking you in. This has to end."

Willow lifted the musket. "And how exactly do you plan on doing that?"

"Everywhere you go, you leave a trail of death. Aren't you tired?" Val asked.

She didn't answer.

"Don't you want more? Don't you want a life?"

Madrick wasn't sure what he was looking at or what was transpiring. He was usually really good at figuring things out, but this entire situation had him completely confused. How were both Willow and Val some sort of warriors? Why were they warriors?

"I know this may not be the best time to ask, but what is going on?" he asked.

Both Willow and Val stared at him. Then suddenly, Willow grabbed his arm and pointed the musket into his side.

"Drop your weapon or I will shoot him," she said.

"You won't do that," Val said.

"You don't know me as well as you think you do," Willow said. "But you, oh, you are quite transparent."

"What are you talking about?"

"You are completely in love with him, aren't you? Don't even try to deny it. For I see the way you look at him," Willow said.

Val didn't respond.

"I can't say that I blame you. He is remarkable. He is the greatest man I have ever met. And since I know you agree with me, I know you would rather let me go free than let a single hair on his body be harmed."

Val still didn't respond.

"So here is what is going to happen. You are going to let both of us walk out of here and into my guster. Once I am off-planet, I will send Madrick back to AiJalon." Willow paused. "That is unless he chooses to stay with me. He wants to marry me, you know. He told me himself."

Val still didn't respond. But she started to get an odd look in her eyes. Seconds later, Madrick determined why.

After a loud thunk, Willow's body went limp. He turned around to see his sister holding a large oxygen tank in her hands with which she had just clunked Willow over the head.

Elsinor dropped it and said, "I got tired of waiting in the guster."

# Chapter 32

Val had only been in an AiJalonian detention center once before. It was to rescue a young girl named Gess who had fought off her attacker and was arrested for public violence. The case was dismissed but not before Val had to spend the evening fighting for her freedom. It was a rather simple case with no complications, but Val felt that even one night in detention was too long for this girl under the circumstances.

The detention center of course was much nicer than the intergalactic prison. And Madrick was well cared for in his detainment pod, but just like Gess, he didn't deserve to be there. He, too, had been through a traumatic event. His heart was still probably aching over Willow's betrayal. Val desperately wanted to hold him in her arms and tell him that she'd love him more than Willow ever could.

Val stopped pacing the cold, gray waiting room and pressed her eyes shut. She had to rid herself of these irrational, emotional thoughts. It would get her nowhere. She needed to focus on Madrick's release.

There were very few attorneys on the planet given that there was rarely a need for them. The presence of the intergalactic police was enough to stave off criminal activity, but during the last few decades the need for an entire court system grew which included the need for attorneys. Of course, any defendant could request a well-trained attorney from another planet, but the AiJalonian court system favored attorneys of their own species. Thus, it was in Madrick's best interest to find a pure AiJalonian to represent him in his defense. Thankfully, Val was well acquainted with the cousin of one of those few and far between lawyers.

"There has been a slight complication in your friend's case," Font's cousin FlintRoy said two days after the incident.

"What do you mean?" Val asked.

FlintRoy gestured for Val to take a seat. "I'd rather stand, thank you."

"Very well, I will sit." FlintRoy tried to make himself comfortable in the very uncomfortable seating provided in the detention center waiting room. Val was well aware how uncomfortable the chairs were. Madrick's first night in custody, Val had slept in the waiting room. The second night she opted for a hotel room.

"Tell me what has happened," Val said.

"Willow escaped last night."

"What? How? Why did I not hear of this?"

"It is not something the authorities would like to be public knowledge. It is quite embarrassing for them. Apparently, she merely convinced a guard to let her out. They are not ruling out some sort of foul play."

"Let me guess," Val said. "The guard claims he had to do it. He had no control."

"Why, yes. That is exactly what he said."

Val cursed in Minnithian and began pacing. "Complice."

"What?"

"Complice is a drug she often uses on her victims. A very powerful hypnotic. I should have seen this coming."

FlintRoy sighed. "I was hoping, perhaps with your influence, we could convince her to testify to Madrick's innocence. The court is much more likely to believe an AiJalonian."

Not wanting to dwell on the setback, Val said, "So what do we do now?"

"Well, it should still be a relatively simple case. Given the security footage from the hotel, it is quite evident that Madrick Dashing had nothing to do with Leaven CoZark's murder. The only reason he is even being detained is because the general assumption is that he has been working with Miss King."

"General assumption?" Val said, still pacing the room. "They only believe that because he's human. And now Willow is gone. She was the only who could clear him. Gaion, why didn't I see this coming!"

"Don't blame yourself. Though the Ministry of Justice most likely will not believe the testimony of a human, we—"

"So what are we going to do?" Val asked, interrupting him. "We can't leave him here. Tomorrow he'll be transferred to prison."

"You didn't let me finish," FlintRoy said. "I think we have a good chance of having all charges dismissed."

"But you just said they won't believe a human."

"And we will use that to our advantage. Humans have a long history of lying. Thus, their own culture developed a device called a lie detector. By the end of the twenty-third century, they had been improved to the point of 98.7% accuracy. I am having one sent here as we speak."

"So, all we have to do is get Madrick to use this lie detector device and he will be set free."

FlintRoy nodded again. "Thankfully, AiJalonians are more apt to believe a machine than a human."

***

"I honestly cannot believe your half-brother was involved in a murder," Femili said.

"Well, in all honesty," Bragley Dashing said, "the decision from the Ministry of Justice was that he wasn't actually involved. He was just in the wrong place at the wrong time. It was all Willow King's doing actually."

Femili gave her husband a look bordering on shock and confusion. Did he really just dispute her? He did not really just dispute her!

"In fact, he was released after just two days in detention. Usually, any human charged with a crime is either immediately and irrevocably incarcerated in an intergalactic prison or sent directly to a paedor. It is highly unlikely that any AiJalonian court would simply release a guilty human."

Femili continued to stare at her husband.

"But," Bragley said, acquiescing, "given his human nature, he surely had some hand in it. No doubt."

"Yes, no doubt." Femili was pacified by his acquiescence. "In any case, he is completely ruined. He may as well go live in a paedor finally. It is obviously where he belongs. He has already completely ruined the chances for his sisters to marry well. I mean, really, who on AiJalon would want to marry into a family of criminals?"

"You are quite right dear."

"Of course I am right. I can't believe we have to share a name with them. We should have FORCED them to live in the paedors. Then maybe all of this could have been avoided. That should somehow be added into law. We, as an AiJalonian people, should be able to make decisions for the humans. We know what is best for them, much better than they do.

"You are quite right, my dear. But I do feel a little responsible."

Femili looked at him quizzically. "Responsible? How could you be responsible in any way? You had nothing to do with this."

"Well, he is my brother—"

"Half."

"He is my half-brother," Bragley corrected, "and I did make a promise to my father."

"A promise that I am sure he would have dispensed if he knew his child was a murderous criminal."

"But all of this perhaps could have been avoided if I had helped them as I said I would. Perhaps he needed my guidance and I wasn't there to give it. Maybe I should make myself more available to my half-sisters in order to avoid the same thing happening to them."

Femili began to panic. Well, as much as an AiJalonian could panic, that is. She felt she knew the direction of this conversation and didn't like its course. Her big-hearted but small-brained husband was probably going to offer to have Elsinor and Mahogany stay with them for a while so he could offer them guidance through this tragedy. She had to figure out a way to steer this situation in the direction she preferred.

"My dear, do you remember the Satterly sisters?"

"Yes, but I don't see what that has to do with—"

"Well, I have invited them to stay with us for a while."

"You have? Why?"

So that you can't invite your sisters to stay with us, she thought. But instead she said, "Oh, you know me dear, always trying to help those who are less fortunate than ourselves."

"Hmm," Bragley said noticeably confused. "Well, since we already have visitors coming, I can't very well invite more. Our droids are only equipped to service a certain number of people."

"Yes, my dear, it would be too much of a drain. You can invite your sisters some other season. They most likely want this time together anyway."

# Chapter 33

Though Madrick was released from detention, he was under forty-eight hour surveillance before he was free to move about the planet. Any infractions within that time period would mean immediate transferal to an intergalactic prison. Thus, he returned to Mrs. Jensent's home in Cosmo and retreated to his room where he refused to see or speak to anyone save his older sister Elsinor.

For her part, Elsinor did her best to seem compassionate and composed so as to not upset her brother even more. He suffered greatly. Either Willow truly loved him, but still framed him for murder and left him to face AiJalonian justice alone, or she never really loved him at all. Both thoughts had to be incredibly painful for him.

Elsinor welcomed any distraction from her brother's predicament. Well, almost any.

"Can you believe Femili invited Anna and me to stay with them for the rest of the season?" Lace asked Elsinor the day after Madrick's release.

"No, I cannot," was her only response.

"I think it is all because of what happened the night of the hafenstat game."

"Oh? How so?"

"Of course you saw what happened that night!" Lace exclaimed.

"What do you mean?" Elsinor was slightly afraid that Lace was referring to Madrick somehow. But part of her knew that Lace was really only ever concerned with Lace.

"I mean the way Femili and Mrs. Fyatt treated me."

Relieved, Elsinor said, "Yes, they were very civil."

"Civil? Civil! I saw a great deal more than civility. I felt as if I was almost part of the family already."

"Perhaps it is a good thing that they are not aware of your engagement to Edgar."

"Oh no, you will not spoil this for me. The Fyatts obviously have an inclination for me and I will not let you spoil that fact."

"Fine, I won't. But perhaps Miss Amelia Morton will."

"Whatever do you mean?"

"I mean that it seems quite obvious that Mrs. Fyatt intends to arrange a marriage between Miss Morton and Edgar."

"What? Do you really think so?"

"Yes, I do."

"Well it cannot be. He is promised to me and no one else."

As Lace and Elsinor sat, a droid entered the room, announcing the arrival of one Mr. Edgar Fyatt. Elsinor wanted to fall into a hole and disappear but that would not have been appropriate. Instead, she calmed her emotions, stood and prepared to greet Edgar in the most casual way possible.

Edgar stood in the doorway and stared at Elsinor in silence for a moment as if drinking her in. Elsinor wanted to say something immediately but found that she couldn't find the words. Just the sight of him had transfixed her.

Finally, Edgar stepped into the room and said, "Elsinor, how I've longed to—"

"Edgar, I'm sure you know Lace," she said, interrupting him before he said anything that might have embarrassed them both.

Turning to his left he said, "Ah, L—lace S—Satterly." He paused, looked back at Elsinor. "Yes, of course."

Elsinor noticed how his stutter was suddenly more pronounced in the presence of Lace. Edgar never stuttered when they were alone. Somehow, knowledge of this fact was enough to give her a measure of solace. Elsinor realized that apparently she was the only woman on the planet that made him comfortable. Yes, he might be promised to Lace, but she was the one he really loved.

"What is ... " Edgar began.

"Lace and I have struck up an acquaintance of sorts." Elsinor answered the question before it was even asked. "She has confided in me quite a great deal of information."

"Ah, I see," was all Edgar said. In those few words, they both understood the situation. Edgar knew that Elsinor knew the truth about his engagement to Lace. And Elsinor knew that he didn't really want to be engaged to her. It was quite obvious in the fact that Elsinor was the first person he had come to visit even though he knew full well that Lace was also in the city.

"Eddie? Is that you?" Madrick said entering the room. He took one look at Edgar and then embraced him. It was quite the human move. AiJalonian men did not embrace each other in hugs. In that moment, however, Madrick did not care about traditional AiJalonian social constructs. He just wanted a hug from his friend.

"How are you?" Edgar asked, returning the embrace. Though he was surprised by the overt display of affection, he did not rebuke it. He could tell it was something Madrick apparently needed and he didn't want to disappoint yet another Dashing. "I have heard of your troubles and offer my deepest condolences. I cannot imagine what you have been through."

Madrick nodded. "I would rather not speak of it," Madrick said, releasing Edgar and stepping back. "But who cares about me anyway? Elsie has been waiting for you for days."

"Madrick, don't," Elsinor rebuked.

"So sorry I haven't ... been able to visit. I have been otherwise ... en—engaged." Edgar looked back and forth between Elsinor and Lace.

"Otherwise engaged?" Madrick slapped Edgar on the back. "Don't be ridiculous."

"Madrick, if Edgar says he had prior commitments, we must take him at his word."

"Yes, because a man's word is everything," Lace said, speaking up for the first time.

Madrick, not knowing the true situation between Edgar and the two ladies in the room, mistakenly thought that Lace was insulting him. "What is that supposed to mean?" he asked. "Are you referring to my current legal troubles? I did not—"

"Madrick," Elsinor said, interrupting her brother. "Not everything is about you."

Madrick's anger slipped into confusion. He had no idea what was really happening, but he trusted his sister's judgment and relinquished his offense.

An awkward silence filled the room.

"Well, I must be going," Edgar said suddenly.

"Yes," was all Elsinor said.

"Already? But you just got here," Madrick said.

"I am promised to my sister," he added.

"Well, if you are going to Femili's home perhaps you will escort me. She is expecting me as well," Lace said.

Edgar looked over at Lace for what was only the second time since he entered the home. "Yes, of c—course," he said obviously uncomfortable.

Lace stood and linked her arm in Edgar's. "Madrick," he said with a nod. Looking at Elsinor, he seemed to have lost his voice. He was not even able to voice her name. "El ... " he began and had to stop as his voice cracked. After two attempts, he gave up and just nodded in her direction before leading Lace out of the room.

"What was that about?" Madrick asked once they were gone.

"I don't know what you mean."

"Really? Because both of you seemed rather off."

Elsinor didn't respond.

"Is it because of me? Did he not stay because I'm a criminal?"

"First of all, you are not a criminal. Second, he didn't stay because he was promised elsewhere. It is as simple as that."

# Chapter 34

Of the Satterly sisters, Anna considered herself the forgotten one. She wasn't as pretty, or as dark or as tall as her sister Lace. She felt she never had anything interesting to say and thus most often just said the flat-out wrong or inappropriate thing. She didn't inherit enough AiJalonian genes to make her fit into that culture as seamless as her sister Lace. But she was in no way jealous of her older sister. No, she treasured the gifts that Gaion had bestowed upon Lace. She knew they would prove to be a blessing for both of them. And they already had. Why they had been invited to stay an entire season in Cosmo with the Fyatts! Three months. Surely, in three months and with the endorsement of such a rich family, Anna would be able to find an AiJalonian mate. Maybe not one as eligible or attractive as Edgar Fyatt, but surely someone of similar breeding and financial stability.

Anna could barely contain her excitement one afternoon as she sat in the reading room of the Fyatt-Dashing home with none other than Mrs. Fyatt and Mrs. Fyatt Dashing. Lace had gone off somewhere scampering about town. Probably looking in shops for her wedding clothes. Oh her sister would make such a beautiful bride! Of course, she would be in the wedding as well. I should be shopping with her, Anna thought. Who would read the tenements of marriage at the wedding? she thought next. What a difficult and boring task.

"Do you know the tenements of marriage in Ancient Ai, Mrs. Dashing?" Anna asked.

Mrs. Dashing looked up from her book, slightly confused. "Yes, I do," she said. "But why are you wondering about the tenements of marriage? Are you planning on getting married?"

"Me, oh no. I do not currently have a suitor. My sister is sure to be married soon and it is usually a relative that reads the tenements at the ceremony."

Both Mrs. Dashing and Mrs. Fyatt put down their books and stared intently at Anna. She did not notice at first as she returned her attention to her book. Truth be told, she didn't really enjoy reading books written on paper. She found them clunky and unwieldy to hold, but wanting to fit in, she agreed to read one. But now at the end of each page she found herself tapping the paper expecting it to change screens.

"Young Miss Satterly," Femili Fyatt said careful to coat her words with sweetness, "I am not a relative of your sister, Lace, so why would I be reading any tenements at any wedding?"

"Yes, but tradition says it can be a relative of the bride or the groom so it is perfectly acceptable for you to read them." Immediately realizing the terrible mistake she just made, Anna stopped tapping the paper and looked up. Anna cursed in Minnith then said, "I wasn't supposed to say that."

Femili looked at her mother and then back at Anna. "Say what, dear? What were you not supposed to say?"

\*\*\*

Madrick sat next to his sister on the bed as she stared straight ahead not even acknowledging his presence.

"How long have you known?" he asked.

"Only two weeks."

"Only two weeks? You have suffered in silence for two weeks?" He couldn't believe it. Thinking back about what had transpired over the last two weeks, his infatuation with Willow, his arrest, the trial, he couldn't help but feel incredibly selfish. Not once had he asked about his sister's well-being in the past two weeks. They used to be so close. Before

241

Willow, not a day would pass when they wouldn't confide in each other.

Elsinor took a deep breath as if about to say something.

"Stop it, Elsie" he said, interrupting her.

Elsinor turned to look at him, her eyes wide. "What?" she asked.

"Whatever self-deprecating thoughts were creeping into your mind. Stop them."

"But I was just going to say—"

"Shush," he said. "I know what you were going to say. You were going to say something practical and wise. You were going to spout some garbage about things working out the way they should. You were going to try to make me feel better about you feeling bad. You were going to take care of me the way you always do." Madrick wrapped his arms around his sister. "Not this time. I know you love him and I know this hurts. Believe me, I know. So, for once, don't be the adult. Just shut up and cry. Let it out and let me take care of you."

Elsinor needed no further encouragement. She buried her face in her brother's chest and cried.

Elsinor hated crying. She rarely let anyone see her do it. In fact, the only person that had seen her cry before that day was Edgar. That thought made her cry even more. She was determined, however, to overcome this sadness. So even as she cried on

Madrick's shoulder she knew she had to find a way to persevere and carry on.

# Chapter 35

Elsinor tried her best to stay true to her personal vow. She spent the next several days refusing to let Edgar enter mind and did not allow herself to be overtaken yet again by sadness. Her valiant efforts began to succeed. Within a week she was able to go several hours in a row without Edgar being foremost in her thoughts. But one visit from Val rescinded all of her progress.

"Val, I wasn't expecting you," Elsinor said after the ceremonial bows.

"I apologize for the unannounced visit. I started to merely send a TelEx but decided this was something that may need to be said in person."

"Oh, would you like me to get Madrick?"

"Oh, no ... um ... this actually has more to do with you. Well, somewhat anyway."

\*\*\*

"Elsinor," he said with a deep bow signifying he felt he wasn't worthy to stand in her presence.

"Edgar," she replied.

A pause ensued.

"I called you here because I have good news," Elsinor said, finally.

"Good news?"

"Yes. Good news." Elsinor took a seat and indicated that he should do the same. "A very dear friend of mine," she began, though she could not think how to continue. It was such an odd situation. "Um, perhaps you have heard of her. Valdosta Greer?"

"Yes, I have heard the name but have not had the honor of a formal introduction."

"Yes, well, my dear friend, Valdosta, some of us call her Val. Yes, Val ... she has a proposition for you."

"A proposition?" Edgar repeated with obvious confusion.

"Oh, no, nothing untoward." Elsinor took a deep breath and tried to collect herself. Seeing Edgar in person was proving more difficult than she had expected. Of course, she knew logically that they could never be together, but seeing him in person, sitting mere feet away from him, made her heart hope even against her wishes and logical conclusions. "It's more of a proposal. Let me begin again. My friend, Valdosta Greer, has heard of your predicament and wants to help."

"Wants to help? Me? She wants to help me?"

"Yes. She is a woman of means and is in need of a caretaker for her property in the Broadbend Archipelago."

"A caretaker?"

"Yes, she is often ... off-planet and needs someone to care for the grounds of her home while she is away. Of course, there is no actual physical labor (there are droids for that), but you would be responsible for the droids and for their general upkeep. The appointment comes with a salary and lodging. It is not much but it should be enough for you and your ... bride to carve out a living for yourselves." Elsinor was unable to actually say the name of his bride. If at all possible, she never wanted to have to think about Lace Satterly again. For her own emotional well-being, she hoped Lace and Edgar would live their lives rather far away from her own.

Edgar stood and paced the room in deep contemplation. "So you are telling me," he said finally, "that a woman I have never met is offering me a job and a place to live so that I can marry ... my bride." Edgar was not able to say Lace's name either. Perhaps he was trying to be considerate of Elsinor's feelings.

Elsinor nodded.

"This is quite unbelievable. But I guess when you are involved I suppose anything is possible." He paused, then added, "I assume I have you to thank for this offer."

Rising to her feet, Elsinor protested, "Oh, no, no. You mistake me. I did not petition this request on your behalf at all. Val saw an opportunity to help and she took it. This offer is based solely on your own merit. Though I must agree that she could not have bestowed it on a more ... deserving individual."

Edgar continued to pace the room. Stopping short a few feet in front of her, he asked, "I don't understand why you do not hate me."

Elsinor swallowed her emotion. This was perhaps the last time she would ever see or speak to him. She didn't want it to be marked with tears.

"I have no reason to hate you."

"What? Why not? I think you have every reason to hate me."

Shaking her head she said, "You never deceived me. You never made me a promise you knew you could not keep. And the fact that you are honoring promises you DID make years before meeting me only gives me more reason to—" Elsinor caught herself before the word love slipped out. But she didn't have to say it. The word was felt by all in the room. "Even if I did have reason to hate you," she continued, "I don't think I ever could." Elsinor cleared her throat and checked her emotions. "You, sir, have my friendship and you always will."

"I am very glad for that. You, of course, have mine as well." They stared at each other in silence for a moment before Edgar added, "You don't know how badly I wish things were different."

Elsinor nodded. "Only about half as much as I do."

Edgar took a deep breath. "I wish we could run away together. Leave this planet and all its antiquated traditions and prejudices."

She nodded again but didn't respond. She had already revealed too much of her feelings.

"We could assume new identities," Edgar continued softly. "Live in solitude on a glamorous beach on Lumerca." Elsinor closed her eyes and imagined that beach. Though her eyes were closed, she could feel that he had taken a step closer to her.

Her heart began to race as she too decided to indulge in the fantasy. "Not Lumerca," she said allowing herself to smile slightly. "It's much too expensive there and you have been disowned. We could only afford a modest planet like Minnith or Tentor."

"Ah, yes, Minnith. Why didn't I think of that?" He was now so close to her she could practically hear his heartbeat. "I could become a priest in order to support us financially."

"I would till the land and grow food to sustain us physically." Elsinor opened her eyes and stared into those of her beloved.

Edgar gently brushed his fingertips across the back of her hand. Her entire arm warmed at his touch.

A few seconds more of such close proximity and nothing would have stopped them from fulfilling their dream and running away together.

"My family," Elsinor said suddenly.

Edgar sighed and removed his hand. "You are blessed to have a loving family," he said, turning away. "I must admit, I do not know what that is like." He knew how much she cared about her brother, sister, and mother. He wouldn't be able to take her away from them for a life of living in hiding. She would miss them too much. And then one day she might wake up and realize that he wasn't enough for her and want to be with her family again. He couldn't handle losing her after having her for so long. No, this was better for everyone.

"Edgar," she began.

"Don't. There is nothing left to say." He still did not turn and look at her. He wasn't strong enough. Without another word, he left the room.

"Goodbye, my love," she said to no one at all.

# Chapter 36

Madrick did an excellent job of pretending he was all right. He smiled when necessary, joked when expected, and generally acted the way he always had. But it was all an act and Elsinor knew that something wasn't right about her brother. Unfortunately, this feeling was proven true less than a week after the eldest Dashings returned to Haran.

Madrick didn't know why he found himself walking to Willow's home that day. He knew she wouldn't be there. Honestly, he didn't want her to be there. But he still needed to go. Something inside of him needed to say goodbye. Willow's home was locked, of course, but he knew enough about her and about the mechanics of a home security system in order to get past it.

He missed her. Deeply. Even knowing the truth about her. Even knowing she left him to take the fall for a murder charge. He still missed her. He missed the feel of her fingers in his hand; he missed the warmth of her body pressed against his; he missed the feel of her lips. Part of him loved her and always would. A larger part of him, however, realized that her departure to another planet and out of his life was for the best. So why did he find himself in her sitting room reveling in the smell of lavender that had always defined Willow?

Standing, Madrick shook his head. He had to get over her. And what happened next surely reaffirmed that.

***

It was beyond her control. She couldn't help it. Valdosta Greer could not help spending the majority of every day thinking of a way to visit the Dashings in order to see Madrick. It was slightly sad and she hoped the Dashings hadn't realized what she was doing. She assumed they did, but she didn't care. She needed to see him.

After yet another excuse to sit at the Dashing home, Val asked, "So how is your brother doing?"

Elsinor sighed. "He puts on a brave front. He tries to act like everything is normal—as if he is normal again—but I feel he is deeply affected. He hasn't had much success in the way of love."

"What do you mean?"

"I am sure you have noticed how gorgeous he is."

Val hoped Elsinor didn't expect an actual response as she was too flushed at the thought of his looks in order to answer appropriately.

"Well," Elsinor continued, "other women have noticed as well. But because he is half-human, no woman has been sincere in this interest of him."

"I am sorry to hear that." Val wanted to say more. She wanted to say that her interest in him was more than sincere.

"In any case," Elsinor continued, "he may not show it, but he is in a lot of pain. He has taken to wandering off on long walks by himself. He won't even ride his duster anymore. Today for example, he left at first sun and hasn't been back since."

"He left at first sun?" Val asked. That would mean he had already been gone for eight hours. "Has he ever been gone that long before?"

Elsinor thought for a moment. "Actually, no. He usually comes home in four or five hours to eat something."

Val stood and paced the room.

"Should I be worried about him?"

Val wanted to say no. She willed herself to say it, but instead she said, "Yes."

"Why? What's wrong? What do you know?"

"I don't know anything, but I can feel it." Val sighed.

"Feel it?"

Val pulled out her receiver. After pressing a few buttons, she said, "We need to go. Now!"

***

"Maddie, can you hear me?"

He heard his sister's voice but for some reason he couldn't respond.

"Maddie, please answer me. Can you hear me?"

"He won't be able to respond," Val said. "I had to put him in parafrost in order to stop his internal bleeding."

"What happened to him?"

Madrick wanted to answer this question as well. He wanted to tell them that he had been attacked while in Willow's house, but he couldn't.

"My guess?" Val said. "This was CoZark's men."

"CoZark? But why?" Elsinor asked. "How would they even know he was there?"

"They wouldn't. They were after Willow. They probably had surveillance set up at her home in case she ever returned. He was at the wrong place at the wrong time."

"Willow. Again. Gaion, when will she stop hurting him?"

Madrick felt trapped inside his own body. He could neither move nor speak, simply observe the interaction between Val and his sister. Val. Coming to his rescue once again.

"Where are we going?" Elsinor asked.

"I know a talented yet discreet doctor on Oroton 4. He may be able to save his life."

"Oroton 4? We're leaving the planet?"

"Yes, we have to. AiJalon does not have the necessary equipment to deal with Madrick's extensive injuries. Ideally, we would go to Lumerca proper, but it is too far. I am afraid he would not survive the journey."

"Oh Gaion!"

"Jason Barvery used to be a doctor on Lumerca. He can save him."

"But ... But how are we going to get off-planet? Madrick is a human and an ex-prisoner. How will we get the necessary documents to get through the checkpoint?"

"I have friends in high places."

\*\*\*

Madrick's eyes blinked open. A soft light filled his senses.

"Where am I?" he asked.

Rushing to his side, Elsinor said, "Thank Gaion. Maddie, I missed you so much."

"Missed me? Where was I?"

"You have been in a coma for three days while your body healed." Elsinor pulled up a chair next to her brother. "What is the last thing you remember?"

"I was at Willow's home," Madrick began. "They were lying in wait."

"Who, Madrick?"

"I'm not sure. I think I recognized them from the prisoner transport vessel in Cosmo, but I can't be sure."

Elsinor nodded. "That is what we suspected."

After looking around at unfamiliar surroundings—the stark white walls and the blindingly bright light—Madrick asked, "Where are we?"

"Oroton 4."

"No, seriously. Where are we?"

"Seriously. We are on Oroton 4."

"What ... How...Why are we on a Lumercan moon?"

"Your injuries were extensive. Three broken ribs, a crushed skull, collapsed lung, and punctured liver, spleen and large intestine. And that is just what I recall. For a while, we didn't think—" Elsinor paused to collect herself. She obviously wanted to give the appearance of strength to her injured brother. "You almost died, dearest. If you had died,

Madrick, I don't think I could—" Elsinor could no longer hold back her emotion.

"Elsie, Elsie," Madrick said while rubbing his sister's back as she cried on his chest. "I didn't die. I'm fine." He said this even though he couldn't be absolutely sure about the current state of his health. He knew he felt fine. Remarkably well, actually. But the list of injuries that his sister had just rattled off had made that seem impossible. Given his condition, the doctors undoubtedly would have had to grow and implant several organs for him. He wondered how it was all possible. How did they get to a moon? And who was paying for it? As if Gaion himself had willed it, the answer walked right through the door.

"It's good to see you," Val said. "Conscious. It's good to see you conscious, Madrick," she added as if she were afraid to admit she was happy to see him.

He knew the truth. He could feel it. Val was his savior yet again. She had undoubtedly found him unconscious and dying, perhaps even besting the villains who had set upon him. Then, through her own personal wealth and influence, she managed to relocate him to a remote moon where he could receive the necessary medical care to save his life. All this for him. Gaion above, what manner of woman was this? He didn't deserve to even breathe the same air as her, let alone have her save his life.

"Val." Though short of breath and weak, Madrick held out his hand to her. Slowly, she reached out and grabbed it with her own. "Thank you," he said before slipping back into a deep sleep.

# Chapter 37

"Val? Where are you going?" Elsinor asked as she rushed to catch up to her friend. Val seemed determined to exit the hospital as quickly as possible and Elsinor struggled to keep pace with her. The fact that Elsinor was still clothed in an elaborate island dress while Val wore linen pants and a vest did not aid the situation.

"I have to get out of here," Val said.

"You're leaving? But how—"

"Not forever. Just a little while. I have to ... I need to." Val paused and took a breath. "I can't be around him right now. I need to get out for a while. Maybe take a quick trip around the sun or something."

"Why?"

Staring at her hand, Val said, "I went to talk to him. To Madrick. I thought I helped him because it was the right thing to do. It was simply something I would do for anyone who was in need. But then he touched my hand." Val closed her eyes and shook her head. "I am being foolish. I have no reason to hope." Val pressed the button to depressurize the airlock that led to where her guster was docked.

"Do you need company? Do you want to talk or anything?" Elsinor offered. "I believe I know a thing or two about unrequited love.

Val shook her head. "I need to be alone," she said before stepping through.

Elsinor watched as Val stepped through the air lock and waited for the pressurization shift before boarding her guster.

"Gaion, I thought she'd never leave," a voice said from behind.

Elsinor turned around and stared straight in the face of Willow King.

\*\*\*

"What are you doing here, Willow?"

"How is he?" Willow asked in response.

"I asked you a question. Why are you here?"

Willow and Elsinor entered into a staring match of wills, neither wanting to seem weak.

"I don't have time for this," Elsinor said finally as she brushed past her.

"Elsinor, wait."

Elsinor truly never wanted to see or speak to Willow King again. But for some reason she did.

"Why are you here, Willow? Why do you care what happens to him?"

"Because I love him."

Elsinor was both surprised and annoyed at her candor. "You love him? You dare claim to love him? You framed him for murder. You left him, a human, all alone to stand trial in an AiJalonian court for something you yourself did. And you have the audacity to profess your love for him? Lady, if that is love I shudder to think of what hate looks like from you."

"You should," Willow responded severely. "You have no idea what I am capable of."

At this point, Elsinor knew what she was supposed to do. The sensible thing would be to diffuse the situation, to cower in fear of a known murderer and deliver the information she requested. But she was tired of being the sensible one. Her sensibilities had been all but paralyzed by the sight of nearly watching her brother die in her arms. It was a sight she would never be able to purge from her mind. A sight that could have been completely avoided if he had never met one Willow King. This woman had caused her brother nothing but pain from literally the first impact of their initial meeting. This torturous dance of emotion between the two had to end.

Elsinor smiled sweetly as an uncharacteristic surge of courage lined her spine. "You listen to me,

Willow King. When it comes to Madrick Dashing, only Gaion himself knows what I am capable of. So I suggest you leave this facility and this moon before—"

"Before what?" Willow asked, interrupting her. "What on heaven and AiJalon do you think you can do to me? You have no weapon and you definitely cannot defeat me in hand-to-hand combat."

"Perhaps. But what I CAN do is call the intergalactic police. And that is exactly what I did three minutes ago as soon as I heard your sickening voice." Elsinor pulled a small, glowing device out of her pocket. "You might not recognize this contraption," Elsinor said, growing more confident by the second. "It's something Madrick whipped up after that fiasco in Cosmo. He was afraid for our safety so he created this device that can contact the intergalactic police with the simple press of a button."

Willow nervously looked around, knowing that Madrick was completely capable of doing such a thing. She was probably surveying the exits, planning a quick escape.

"Sure, I didn't know it was you at first, but I had my suspicions and I called them just in case. Given that their average response time is 5 minutes and 43 seconds, I'd say you're running out of time."

A look of defeat fell over Willow's face. It was a look Elsinor was not used to seeing in her. And from the pain hidden behind Willow's eyes, defeat was obviously not an emotion she was used to feeling.

"Fine, I'll go," she said. "Just, please ..." She sighed. "Is he going to live?"

Lights in the hospital began to flash as the menacing alarm indicating a station-wide lockdown blared. The intergalactic police must have initiated it. Suddenly, she regretted calling them. She didn't know what would happen to Willow if she was caught given her record and that she had already previously escaped police custody.

"Elsinor, I swear to Gaion I will stay away from him. I will never put him in harm's way again. Just ... just give me hope."

Elsinor looked into Willow's eyes and said, "He is going to make it."

# Chapter 38

Something had changed inside him toward Val. He wasn't sure what it was and he wasn't sure when it happened. All he knew was that every day he longed to see her. And when he finally did, he felt an indescribable joy. When she went away, there was an ache in his chest that was equal parts pain and desire. Valdosta Greer was anything but the typical proper AiJalonian as he had once thought. She was exciting yet calming, strong but compassionate. She was everything he could ever want in a mate. In fact, she was too good for him. He was a lowly human with a shadow of criminal activity that would forever hang upon him. There was no way Valdosta Greer would ever have him. But that didn't mean he wouldn't try to convince her.

Valdosta and Madrick had been prone to playing music together as of late. While each loved the company of Elsinor, they had both noticed her recent predilection for solitude. Due to the way things ended with Edgar, Madrick knew his sister needed time to heal with her emotions. And he also knew she preferred to deal with those emotions in private. He would not impose upon her until she wished it.

It was during one of these impromptu music sessions when Madrick had an epiphany. He stopped playing the bandalore and looked over at Val on the ziln.

"Is something the matter?" she asked when she realized he had stopped playing.

"Yes. No." He set down the bandalore and walked over to her.

"Are you in pain?" Her eyes grew large with worry.

"Yes."

"I knew we shouldn't have left Oroton 4 so soon. Shall I summon a medical droid? We have pain suppressants."

"No, it's not that kind of pain." He paused.

Val looked at him, confused.

"Val," he said, taking her hands away from the ziln and placing them between his own. "Val," he said again, hesitantly.

He wanted to say flat out that he loved her but looking into her eyes, her beautiful dark eyes, he lost confidence. If only he knew for sure how she felt about him. Still holding both her hands, Madrick lifted her from her seat. Once her face was mere inches from his he said, "Do you remember when we were in the prisoner transport vehicle?"

Val diverted her eyes. "Of course, I do," she said, obviously trying not to look at him.

Madrick lifted her chin with his finger in order to see her eyes. "Willow held a musket to me. And she said you wouldn't let me die because ... because you love me."

"Madrick, I—" Val tried to break free from his grasp but he pulled her to him. With his body placed close against hers, he kissed her. He meant it to be a brief brush of the lips to shock her into telling him the truth. But he found that once her lips touched his, he didn't want the feeling to stop. His entire body tingled and a sensation enflamed him, a fire that could only be quenched with more Val. He wrapped his arms around her body and pressed her closer to him until they were almost one unit.

Once he had kissed her to satisfaction, he pulled away slightly, smiled, and said, "What say you now? Do you love me?"

"I ... I ..." she stuttered as if searching for words.

"Lie to me and I shall be forced to kiss you again."

Smiling, she placed her arms around his neck, "In that case, the answer is no."

"Like most AiJalonians, I find you to be a completely incompetent liar. Thankfully, you can compensate with your kissing expertise."

He kissed her again, slowly, deeply. Though it was impossible for her to doubt his feelings for her at this point, he decided he should make them clear.

"I love you, Valdosta Greer. It took a while to realize it, but now that I do, I know that I need you near me. I need you in my life. I need to make you happy. I need to see you smile, and probably most importantly, I need to feel you, touch you, and kiss you, as often as possible. I know I'm human and I can't offer you much—"

"Don't say that," Val said, putting her fingers over his lips. "You are exquisite. You are perfect and I love you more than any words could ever express."

"So you'll marry me?"

"Of course."

Though Madrick was exquisitely happy at the prospect of spending the rest of his life with Val, he didn't want to tell his sister. He knew she was still suffering at the thought of Edgar. He hated the fact that he would be so happy when his sister wouldn't be. She, of all people, deserved happiness.

# Chapter 39

"You have certainly been happy lately," Elsinor said to her brother one morning.

His smile faded. "I'm sorry, Elsie. Do you want me to stop?"

"Stop being happy? Why on AiJalon would I want that?"

"Because you are so unhappy."

"What makes you think ... ? Why would I be ... ?" Elsinor paused, realizing those were silly questions. She knew exactly why her family would think she was unhappy. She thought she had done a good job of hiding her true feelings but apparently not. At this moment she despised her human tendencies and wished she had more AiJalonian blood in her. Maybe then she would be able to conceal her true feelings better. "Madrick, dear, I am happy. I am." At least her humanity allowed her to lie convincingly.

"Really? Truly?" he asked.

"Yes, of course. I have my family. I have you in good health. I have everything I need." Elsinor kissed her younger brother on the cheek tenderly.

Smiling, Madrick set down his bandalore. "In that case, I have news."

Turning to her brother she gave him her full attention.

"It's about Val. We are getting married."

"Married?"

"You're upset, aren't you?"

"Gaion no, Maddie. I'm just a little surprised. I mean I knew you liked her. From almost your first meeting you showed you were compatible. You both have the same wicked sense of humor. I just didn't know you were quite over Willow King."

"I am. Trust me. I am quite over Willow. My whole obsession with her was ludicrous. It was nothing more than infatuation. I didn't really know her. And once I had my feelings for her in check, once I saw the true Willow King, I realized there was no way I could love her the way I love Val."

"Well ... love. You love her?"

"I do. More than I ever thought possible."

Just as Madrick was professing his love for Val and indicating how they would be spending their lives together, Elsinor received a TelEx.

"Who is it?" Madrick asked.

It was as if Gaion was trying to teach her some sort of lesson in suffering and patience. Maybe she was the female version of Boj, the man in the ancient writing who was tested by the evil one with the death of his family and the affliction of disease. But instead of death, Elsinor was first to suffer the happy marriages of everyone close to her knowing that her one and only opportunity for happiness was forever shattered.

Swallowing her emotions, Elsinor said, "It's from Mrs. Fyatt."

"Edgar's mother?"

"No, his wife."

"Why on AiJalon would she be writing you?" Madrick asked, visibly annoyed and upset. "Dreadful woman. She is relishing in her conquest is she not?"

"I am going to go for a walk."

"I'm sorry, Elsie. I'm so sorry."

"Don't be. Everything is as it should be. There is no reason to be sorry or upset. There is no reason to be anything but content." Once again, she thanked Gaion for the humanity of lying.

Once alone, Elsinor took out her receiver. She didn't know why she was so drawn to actually watching the message from Lace. She should have just deleted it. But there was a morbid curiosity in the whole situation. Part of her just wanted to see a glimpse of Edgar. If he looked happy, maybe she could be at peace with the situation.

Dearest Elsinor,

I just wanted to let you know, dear friend, that I was married this morning! You cannot believe how much of a joy it is to be a married woman. My husband and I send you our best wishes as we leave for our honeymoon today. Oh, if only you could be half as happy as I am one day. Though I don't think it possible. Being Mrs. Fyatt is truly the greatest thing in the galaxy.

Elsinor shut off the receiver. Madrick was right. Lace was a dreadful woman and she couldn't bear to look in her face anymore.

Elsinor walked slowly and thoughtfully back to Barton Domicilio. After spending several hours at the lake, she felt she could now deal with the reality that she would most likely be alone for the rest of her life. Madrick would be off, probably gallivanting about the galaxy with Val. Every day, more and more pure AiJalonian features were revealing themselves in Maggie. In a few years, she would turn into a beautiful young lady and no doubt capture the attention of an eligible AiJalonian. But she, Elsinor Dashing, was doomed to live life as a spinster, perhaps taking care of her mother for the rest of her days.

She sighed. There was nothing wrong with that fate. She could be content with this life.

As she approached the domicilio, Madrick came out to meet her.

"Elsie, where have you been?" he asked.

"Just by the lake thinking. Why?"

"Your receiver is off. I couldn't get in contact with you."

"Yes, I know. I needed some quiet time."

He sighed. "I got a message from Edgar. He is on his way here."

"Here? Why?"

"I do not know but—"

Before Madrick could even finish his sentence, they heard the rumblings of a duster. "And he's here."

As she watched him dismount from his duster, Elsinor felt as if she had suddenly lost the ability to form words. There was so much she wanted to ask. Where was Lace? Why wasn't he on his honeymoon? Were they honeymooning in Haran? Oh Gaion, that had to be it. They were going to honeymoon in Haran as a way to continue this torment of a trial from Gaion himself. Elsinor took a deep breath and steadied herself. She was not going to succumb. This would not break her.

"Elsinor, hello," he said with the ceremonial bow.

"Hey, Eddie," Madrick offered when his sister did not respond. "Do you want to come in?"

Mechanically, Elsinor lead the way into the domicilio. Why on AiJalon would her brother invite him in? The last thing Elsinor wanted to do was spend time discussing his beautiful wedding to his beautiful bride. It was insufferable.

"Edgar?" both Marzi and Maggie said as they entered the parlor. Surely Madrick told them about the TelEx from Lace, thus they must have been equally shocked as to his current presence in their home.

"I know you all must be surprised to see me today," Edgar said a little uneasily.

"We are, of course, always happy to see you," said Marzi, "but on today of all days, we thought you might be a little ... busy."

Edgar looked down at his dust-covered shoes. "Today of all days is the day I needed to see the people who have come to mean the most to me, especially you Elsinor."

"Elsinor?" Madrick asked. "How can you say that? Were you not just hours ago standing before Gaion forever joining two souls? Two souls. One of which was not my sister?"

"Um, yes, that is true but I don't see—"

"How is Lace by the way?" Marzi asked, trying to diffuse the situation.

With a confused expression, Edgar said, "She is fine, I suppose."

"Is she on her way?" Marzi asked

"Where?"

"Here."

"No, why would she be?" he asked.

"For your honeymoon."

"My honeymoon?"

"Yes, didn't you just say that this morning joined two souls together in front of Gaion?" Madrick asked.

"Yes, but one of those souls was not mine."

All the Dashings were uttered speechless as they exchanged confused glances with one another.

Edgar continued, "Once I lost my fortune, I also lost Lace's love."

She realized that Edgar was continuing to speak, but for the life of her she could no longer decipher his words. Her mind was consumed with trying to process what he had just said. Two souls, one of which was not his. Was this possible?

"Wait. What?" Elsinor asked, finding her voice for the first time in several minutes.

Edgar nodded as if he had momentarily lost his own voice as well. "Lace, this morning, married my brother Roymond. Apparently, they had become accustomed to using their CSA's for actions other than ... dancing. And given the fact that I am now penniless and my brother quite rich, Lace asked if she may be released from our engagement in order to marry him. Making her Mrs. Roymond Fyatt," he said finally.

Elsinor stood. "Then you are not married?" she asked.

"No, I am not."

Elsinor audibly gasped as tears streamed down her face. Her knees gave way and she clasped the edge of a chair to keep herself from falling to the ground.

"Is she crying?" Maggie asked. "I have never seen her cry before," she added in a whisper.

The chair proved to be insufficient support and she found herself sinking to the floor, continuing to cry into her hands.

"Oh my Gaion! Edgar's crying too," Maggie said.

"I didn't even now AiJalonians COULD cry," Marzi said.

"I think we should go now," Madrick said.

Once they were alone, Edgar knelt on the floor in front of Elsinor. He took one of her hands in his, letting the other continue to cover her eyes. "I am so sorry I hurt you," he said. "Not by anything I said or did, but by everything I didn't say and didn't do. Everything I couldn't say or couldn't do. So many times I wanted to tell you how I felt about you but I couldn't. I wanted to tell you how you are the most amazing creature I have ever met. I wanted to tell you how you are the only thing that makes me feel comfortable in my own skin."

Elsinor continued to cry. "As I stand before Gaion, dear, dear Elsinor, if I had known that a woman like you existed, I would have waited my entire life to find you. But as it was, boredom and plain stupidity led me to attach myself to the first woman who attempted to draw me in. I wanted to tell you all of these things but I couldn't as I was bound to Lace. But now I'm free. So now I can tell you, I love you, Elsinor Dashing. With all my heart I love you. And if you can ever forgive me—"

"No," she spoke through tears, interrupting him.

"No you can't forgive me?"

"No. Yes."

"I understand if you cannot forgive me," Edgar said.

"No, no. You mistake me," she said, removing her hand from her face and revealing a smile. "I can't forgive you because there is nothing to forgive."

"These are tears of joy not sadness or anger?" he asked.

Instead of responding, she kissed him. "Yes, yes they are."

"Then you still love me? You will marry me?"

"Yes and yes."

# Epilogue

Val wasn't sure if she could ever go back to her old life of crossing the galaxy fighting sexual predators in the hopes of one day finding out the truth about her sister. Yes, that life gave her a sense of fulfillment, but after being married to Madrick for several months, she wasn't sure what was more fulfilling. Her husband filled a need inside of her so completely, at times she wasn't sure if she would ever be able to leave his side for longer than a moment again.

She had all but passed the torch on to the Darkenys as they continued the fight for the freedom of enslaved girls. But there was one thing that could always bring her out of her premature retirement.

Walking down an island beach, Val felt her husband squeeze her hand in his. She loved the feel of his skin against hers; she loved his strength that she could even feel in the tips of his fingers. She loved every single thing about Madrick Dashing. And even though it was slightly unsettling the way people always stared at him, Val had to remind herself that it wasn't because he was human or had a criminal past. It was simply because he was just that good looking.

It was during this particular moment of peace and calm that her world was rocked forever.

Two figures walked down the beach towards them. "Is that ... ? No, it can't be." Val smiled and then quickened her step in order to close the distance to the visitors more quickly. Madrick followed.

"Font, Elloree, what are you doing here?" They started with ceremonial bows but then abandoned them in exchange for hugs. "May I introduce my husband, Madrick Dashing?" she said.

"So nice to meet you," Elloree Darkeny said.

"We apologize for missing the wedding," FontL'Roy said. "We were on a mission."

"I understand," Madrick said with a smile. "How is your little one?"

"Amazing," Elloree said. "He is visiting with my sister Jai in Penuel for a while."

"Though I do enjoy the surprise," Val said, "I suspect there is a particular reason why you are here."

Elloree and Font exchanged glances.

"So, Madrick," Elloree said, "I hear your mother is from Tentor. My mother, too, spent several years there. Perhaps we know people in common." Elloree gestured for them to continue walking down the shore while Val and Font began walking in the other direction.

"What's going on?" Val asked.

Font hesitated.

"It is quite obvious that there is something you wish to tell me."

Font still didn't respond. It was as if he was trying to build up the courage to say what he needed to say.

"It is about my sister, isn't it?" Val stopped walking. "She's dead, isn't she?"

"No, not at all. Quite the opposite," he said.

"What?"

"Dahlonega Greer is alive and we found her."

### ###

# Author's Note

Thank you for taking the time to read Sense and Sensibility in Space. As an independent author, the most effective way to promote my book is through word of mouth. So if you enjoyed my work, please tell a friend and consider leaving a review. Thanks!

# Coming Soon

# Mansfield Park
# IN SPACE